I0700598

Banana
Brain

ISBN (paperback): 978-1-959153-16-0
ISBN (eBook): 978-1-959153-17-7

Printed in the United States of America.

Designed and published by Albatross Book Co.
www.albatrossbookco.com

Banana Brain

C. S. FRITZ

For Phil,
who fathered what another abandoned.
From within the deepest part of me, thank you.

Other works

by C. S. Fritz

A Fig for All the Devils

All Creatures Living Beneath the Sun

Cabbage

Enjoy this author-curated playlist as you read.

Banana Brain

buh-NA-nuh brayn

Scatterbrained, silly, irrational, or losing their grip mentally.

New Message
Cancel
q w e r t y u i o p
a s d f g h j k l
z x c v b n m
space

The chimpanzee dragged Lena through the tall, yellowing grass by her hair like a hunter dragging its kill. Her screams were swallowed by the early morning fog that lingered after the desert monsoons. It was too early for witnesses, too far for mercy. The creature's strength made her body feel weightless, her limbs flopping behind her as tufts of her scalp peeled away under its death grip. Hot blood poured down her neck in rivulets, soaking into the already red soil.

Her voice cracked as she cried out, the syllables catching and collapsing like glass in her throat. But only the cold-blooded reptiles and nocturnals heard her. The world was silent, the gods were silent. No one cared.

Somewhere in the spinning agony, she thought of her grandson's birthday this weekend; he'd be three. Just a cake, some candles. The birthday song felt like acid. Guilt for saying no to babysitting, guilt for all that she should have done penetrated her like a spreading fire. Her ribs scraped over the yellow rocks like red chalk; her body dragged across gritty concrete and forgotten zoo paths. The chimpanzee was pulling her not to kill her, but to keep her. To play.

She could feel the guilt swell larger than the pain. It bloomed like something infected in her chest. Her mouth filled with the taste of it, sulfur and fire, like licking ash.

At last, the chimp stopped in the old abandoned and overgrown antelope field. A dead place. The chimpanzee grew to like it here.

Lena collapsed, twitching, barely alive. Her eyes fluttered open. The animal sat against an Alligator Juniper tree, silent, regal, studying her like a king bored with his concubine. She sobbed, whispering, "Please . . . please, God, don't let me die . . ."

The chimp didn't twitch under her pleas. Her cries were like sugar on its black tongue.

Then the animal moved.

Without warning, it tore up fistfuls of poison ivy and began shoving them down her throat. Poisonous vines, leaves, and hairy stems. Each packed like meat into a grinder. Lena thrashed and gagged, her throat flayed raw as the chimp's arm kept going. Deeper. Deeper still. Past her tongue. Past the barrier of flesh. Until it touched something no creature should. It touched her heart. Her body bucked under the pain, as her screams collapsed into clotted whimpers. The animal didn't stop. Wouldn't stop. The chimpanzee perched on her stomach like a roosting vulture, gazing down at her with stoic curiosity, pawing at her face like a child picking through a toy chest. He tugged her ear from her skull like a rose petal, flicked it between his fingers, then moved on. Eyelids. Bottom lip. Her Adam's apple . . . each ripped with the soft sound of gum tearing from carpet.

Now and again, the chimp looked around to see if anyone was watching or coming, only to return to his new knick-knack.

Lena was in and out of consciousness, but every time she would head toward the blackness, the chimp would pound on her face and chest, awakening her for more. Like it wanted her lucid, eyes wide open, as her death stepped out from the wings and took the main stage.

He bit her fingers one by one until they snapped. Tore at her clothes. Licked the salt and blood from her trembling skin like it was jungle nectar.

Then, something even stranger.

Just before the final blow, the chimpanzee reached into the grass and picked up a cell phone. A fucking iPhone 14 with a black case and cracked gorilla glass. And, grabbing Lena's broken jaw, he stretched her lips with his fingers into a grotesque smile.

Looking through the purple blood that filled her eyes, she saw the chimp smiling. The two of them, smiling at each other. Then the animal took a photo of her face, working the mechanics of the phone with the efficiency of a teenage girl—swiping, clicking, and framing her like a professional photographer.

Lena moaned, losing more breath as a vignette of darkness circled her vision. The world spun as hell opened its gates to welcome her in. Her last sight was the chimp lifting a bloody finger to its lips and whispering, "Shhh."

Then . . . click, the last photo of her life.

Part 1

Chapter 1

"Adam, this is our final court-ordered session. Is there anything remaining you'd like to discuss?" the counselor asked, adjusting herself in her collapsing office chair. Everything in the room looked like it had been abandoned by someone with better insurance. Cheap wood grain laminate, a bookshelf that leaned like it wanted to die, the kind of plastic blinds that snapped if you gave them a good yank. To Adam, this wasn't an office; it was his holding cell with fluorescent lighting.

Adam slowly raised his face, the weight of the hour dragging on his jaw. He sat in silence for a few seconds, then exhaled like someone choosing the method of his own execution.

"Well," he said, "I keep having this recurring vision."

She perked up, hopeful. "Go on."

He gave her a smile that didn't reach his eyes. "I keep having this crazy vision, where I'm not the patient. You are. I take notes about your pain, but say nothing, and nod at the deaths in your life. I pretend while giving zero fucks."

The counselor's jaw ticked once. "That's enough, Adam."

"No, I think we're just getting somewhere," Adam said, impersonating her tone and mannerisms. "This has been tremendously helpful. I was court-ordered to open up, you scribbled your horseshit in your yellow pad, and nothing whatsoever changed. But hey, at least one of us walked away with a paycheck."

Her voice dipped into something fragile. "Surely this isn't all you took from our time together?"

Adam laughed, but it wasn't joy. It was a bark of disbelief. "Be careful with your guilt, Adam."

"Yeah? What's that supposed to mean?"

"It means," the counselor replied, "guilt is not a wound. Wounds close and scab over. Guilt is something else. A parasite that wants you to forget it's there. Because if you keep forgetting it long enough, it grows teeth."

"Geez, that's fucking poetic," Adam said, removing eye contact.

"This is my concern for you, Adam. You won't face it. You won't fight for anything. There is something inside you. Something that remembers what you swore to forget. Something that still bleeds for the thing you refuse to talk about."

Adam heard every word of her warning. He knew she was right, but felt amnesia was the best medicine. God, he wanted a drink. He made his decision, and rather than surrendering, he chose violence. "I don't get you!" he snapped, his voice rising. "I try to be honest, and you get nervous, which makes me nervous that I'm blowing my shot to get guardianship over Ruby. Then I say what you and the lawyers want to hear, and I get bitch slapped for manipulating the system. So which one is it,

Brenda? Shit, you want the truth or the version that plays well in court?"

"Fine, tell me this . . . are you still needing to listen to Coldplay to fall asleep?"

The patient had had enough. Adam stood, the cheap pleather couch squeaking like it was glad to be rid of him. His hands shook, not from fear, but from emotional burnout. From holding the line too long in these gatherings.

"I've played your games. I've colored inside your lines. I'm so very tired. Are we done?"

She glanced at the files on her lap, her tone cooled. "Almost. When do you start working with your uncle? I need to update your record. Then you can go, and I'll be available if you ever need me. You or Ruby."

"I just finished training, tomorrow is my first shift," Adam muttered, already reaching into his pants for a cigarette, itching for open air.

"And who will watch Ruby while you're at work?"

"It's a night shift gig. She'll sleep through it. We're good."

"And you're not worried those kinds of hours will make you go a bit bananas?"

Adam placed the unlit cigarette in his mouth and stared at her with something wicked in his face. "Already there, Brenda," he said with a grin, the cigarette hanging from his lip like a white flag, surrendering to the insanity. He stepped toward the door, hand on the knob. Paused. Then, with perfect calm, "Thanks for listening, Brenda. I'm sure it was exhausting pretending to give a shit." He shut the door softly, like closing another casket in his life. He was getting used to that.

"In my place, in my place
Were lines that I couldn't change
I was lost"

Coldplay

Chapter 1

Chapter 2

Prescott, Arizona carries a curse. Not the dramatic, biblical kind with thunder and frogs. No, this one is quieter. Older. It hangs in the air like copper dust, coats the lungs, and settles in the bloodstream. You don't see it at first. You feel it. And once it's in you, it doesn't come out.

Adam felt like the only one who noticed the shadow that hung over the city. The only one who saw the red smear in the sky at dusk, or how the soil bled when it rained. He tried to talk about it once or twice, back in high school. People laughed. Told him to get over himself. He stopped trying to warn anyone after that. He didn't care anymore. He hated this place. And part of hating a cursed town meant hating the people who chose to live in it, like the curse didn't exist.

Prescott's crown jewel is the town square. Four blocks of fake charm. Souvenir shops selling turquoise jewelry nobody wants. Breweries pretending to be Portland. Aztec galleries run by white men in moccasins. In the middle of it all squats the courthouse, a faded southern Gothic-style relic, with wide stone columns and a rot that no renovation could hide. It looked like a plantation house that got lost and never found its way back to Georgia.

Adam's family moved here the summer before his freshman year of high school. He'd been trying to leave ever since. But leaving Prescott wasn't simple. And the longer he lived here, the more he started noticing that no one really came or went. No one showed up with dreams and furniture. Everyone he met was born here. Raised on the same streets, in the same schools, breathing the same poisoned air. No transplants. No newcomers. Just the same faces in slightly older bodies.

There's gravity to cursed places. Not metaphorical. Physical. You feel it in your ankles. In your gut. A low, humming pull that drags you back every time you try to leave. The locals call it "charm." Adam calls it *the suck*. That slow, spiraling drain toward something black and grizzly at the center of town.

That was the part that truly chilled him. It was as if the town didn't allow outsiders. As if it grew its people like crops, with an invisible barrier fence keeping the crops in and the pests out, which always produced a haunting thought for Adam. *Why did the gods allow his family into their territory?*

Beyond the square, it's every other forgotten American town. A dying mall slumped on a hillside like a corpse no one wants to bury. A Taco Bell with cracked windows. Goodwill stores that feel like a hostage situation. Prescott tries to pretend it's something it's not, mostly happy.

Two miles north on highway 89 toward Chino Valley, between the red hills and patches of yellow grass, half hidden behind a row of wind-bent trees, it sits.

The zoo. It's not even a real zoo. It's a hospice for animals no one wanted. A graveyard offering field trips to local schools. Here, the bears melt in the sun. A Siberian tiger paces in a 12x12 cage made of fake grass and rusted bars. And the chimps? The group of invalid primates that spend their time half-heartedly grooming each other, like they're in a perpetual state of mourning? They don't live here. They wait here to die like all residents of Prescott. When Adam was in high school, he pitied the animals beyond the bars. Now, he doesn't give a shit. This is where he works now. This is where everything will be stolen from him. The zoo sells itself as a place of conservation and preservation. In reality, it's none of those things. It's a mouth with fangs. You go in thinking it's a job, a fresh start, something temporary between misery and meaning. But it eats you, digests you, shits you out, and then, somehow, calls you back. To be eaten again.

Fucking Prescott, Arizona.

Because here, nothing gets buried deep enough in the hard red soil. Everything eventually comes crawling back to the surface.

"Those who are dead are not dead;
they're just living in my head"

Coldplay

Chapter 2

Chapter 3

The two of them sat at Peter Piper Pizza, where the carpet smelled like vomit and despair, and the soundscape was all shrieks and scolding. Children scream with joy, parents scream from exhaustion. It was chaos, but it was chaos that Adam and Ruby had come to crave. They liked it here. Not just because a large pizza was $9.99 and tasted like warm cardboard left too close to a radiator, but because this was where families still functioned. Everything in their life now felt like it was moving in slow motion, but here, kids sprinted to their mom's with skinned knees, and dads lifted them overhead like trophies. Every scream from a child was an invitation to remember. Every parental overreaction was a reminder that someone cared enough to correct.

They liked the screaming. Because they needed to remember. It warmed their cold, growing insides like hot cheese. "How's the pizza, cockface?" Ruby asked, tearing the cheese with her teeth like it owed her money.

"Fuck, dude, please stop calling me that or anything else your deranged brain comes up with," Adam said, dabbing grease off his slice with a crumpled napkin. "I know I'm not Dad. But a little respect wouldn't kill you."

"No can do, gov'nor," she said in a cracked British accent, folding her slice like a street taco. That was Ruby. Hedonism and heresy wrapped in a hoodie. If it felt good, it must be right. That was her church doctrine now.

"How'd therapy go today?" She asked it casually, but her eyes flicked up to meet his.

"It's over, so that's good."

"Did she fix us? Solve the riddle of how to resurrect our tragically dead parents?"

"Let's not talk about them right now," Adam protested with a sigh.

Ruby smirked, a slice of pepperoni hanging off her lip like a badge of defiance. "See, that's the thing, Baby Dick. You don't talk about them to hide your pain. I talk about them to hide mine."

"Well," Adam said, sitting up straighter, "talk to yourself then."

"Okay, I will," Ruby leaned back in the cracked, purple booth like a therapist on a couch. "What's your favorite thing that you remember about your dead parents, Ruby?"

"Thanks for asking, Ruby," she said to herself, eyes wide, voice chirpy. "I'd say it's the food fights at Thanksgiving, when Mom started it just to see if Dad would throw mashed pota—"

"That's enough!" Adam slammed his pizza down hard enough to make a kid at the next table cry. His forced smile was instant, panic disguised as composure. He wasn't screaming at a random kid—he wanted the onlookers to know. Just a sibling. Just a guardian failing in public.

Ruby blinked once, wiped her mouth calmly, and took a long sip from her drink. It was Mountain

Dew spiked with lemonade, a concoction she proudly named Dew-Nade, as if branding her beverages gave her control over the growing chaos of her pained life. Then she stood and extended her hand like a business transaction. "Give me some cashola to go beat some kindergarten bitches at air hockey." Adam stared at her palm, the absurdity of the moment sharpening everything. He gave her five bucks like it was a bribe to buy some silence. As she skipped off toward flashing lights and clanging arcade machines, Adam exhaled and leaned back. He pulled out his phone and tapped the photo. The photo. The one he looked at when everything in him wanted to scream. The one hidden in the album that needs a certain face to unlock.

And that's when he heard it, Coldplay.

As if piped in from hell itself, the restaurant speakers dropped the opening piano notes . . .

When you lose something you can't replace.
When you love someone, but it goes to waste.

God, he hated Coldplay ... probably more than God hated Coldplay. And that was saying something.

"Why do all the monsters come out at night?"

Coldplay

Chapter 4

"Adam, this is Daffodil, our newest chimpanzee," his uncle said, flicking on the cold, white fluorescents.

The harsh light poured across the chimp's face, illuminating every crevice and fold in its skin. Adam couldn't tell what was scar tissue and what was simply beast. The creature's black, leathery hide was speckled with wild, cosmic hair, making its features blur into one strange, liquid shape. It was all muscle, all structure. A hulking figure that seemed to force Adam to focus on the parts of it that reflected the light, as if the rest of its mass was avoiding it entirely. Its large fingernails caught the fluorescent glow, gleaming like black beetles. The oily, jutting brow. The hard, bloodless lips. The filthy ears. And then, its eyes . . . those yellow eyes, shimmering as though they were being electrified from somewhere deep within, radiating a chilling, unnatural light.

"Dilly, can you say hi?" his uncle asked the way a father might coax a shy child.

Adam never liked his uncle. In fact, he despised the man, but he had no choice now but to pretend otherwise. He summoned every trick he'd learned in high school theater: Believe what you're saying, nod, but not too much, and other manipulative bullshit.

His uncle bought it. The chimpanzee didn't.

The chimp stared back at Adam with an intensity that felt like it was digging into his skull.

"This thing is freaky. What's wrong with her?" Adam asked, still forcing interest into his voice but wishing he were anywhere else, anywhere other than here, with this creature, in this zoo. Bed. A bar. Hell, even drowning in piss felt more appealing.

"Him, not her," his uncle corrected, repositioning the toothpick in his mouth. Adam had known the man for years, and the toothpick had never once left its place. It was like an extension of his jaw, a permanent wooden fixture.

"Oh, I just thought it was female because of the name . . ." Adam trailed off, almost embarrassed, his gaze shifting uneasily toward the chimp.

"Nope. Just a chimpanzee with a cute name," his uncle said, his tone dripping with the kind of affection Adam could never understand.

"Cute name?" Adam's voice turned sour, his stomach twisting. He couldn't stand the soft, almost effeminate way his uncle spoke. "So, what's wrong with him?"

"Well, that's why he's here," his uncle said, sliding a pair of light blue latex gloves over his hands. Adam watched as the chimp, still unfazed, let his uncle probe him. His fingers grazed across the animal's skin, searching for something of interest. Adam felt his stomach turn. He couldn't help but feel like he was witnessing something invasive, like catching someone undressing through a cracked door.

"He was the last chimp left alive at the sanctuary in Caddo Parish, Louisiana," his uncle continued, probing the chimp's mouth with his thumb, making the animal's lips twitch but not break its gaze. Adam felt uncomfortable, complicit even as he watched.

"I thought sanctuaries kept animals alive?" Adam asked, surprised at his own interest, his voice betraying a hint of genuine concern.

"They do. But some sort of virus or infection took out all of his buddies." He ripped the gloves off with a snap and then pulled out his phone to take a few photos.

"How do we know Dilly doesn't have the virus?" Adam asked, a note of caution threading his voice.

"Because he's alive," his uncle answered, shrugging.

"Yeah, but he was around it, right? Is he immune?"

"Not really sure. But he's healthy for now. And he's here, whether we like it or not."

"Like it or not?" Adam started to grow more curious.

"It doesn't matter, we're just keeping him here until we find him a new home," his uncle finished, grabbing Dilly's hand and leading him toward a cage, its wires glinting like cold teeth in the harsh light. Dilly obediently followed, waiting for his uncle to open the door, feed him, and direct his next move.

"You shouldn't have to worry about him tonight, on your rounds," his uncle said as he secured the lock with a satisfying click. "He's pretty high on meds, should be out for a while. But just in case, it's probably best you avoid this room. His mood may be unpredictable as the drugs wear off."

"Got it. Thanks for the tip." Adam felt his pulse quicken, but tried not to show it.

"Adam . . ." his uncle's voice was suddenly quieter, more serious, " . . . do you want to be here?"

Adam froze, caught off guard by the question. His uncle was staring at him, just like the chimp had. Watching, waiting for something more. But Adam had nothing else to give.

"Not really," Adam replied, his voice hollow, "but I need to be."

His uncle didn't say anything for a moment, just continued staring, his look leaving something unspoken.

"Your grieving process is real," Jeff said finally, his tone oddly soft, "but your sister says it might be good for you to get out of the house for a bit. I agree with her." He placed a hand on Adam's shoulder, but it felt more like a weight than comfort. "Hell, you know the offer still stands that I can take your little sister off your hands to give you a break. Get you back to college and your life." Adam nodded with understanding, but wouldn't dream of it.

"Oh, and one more thing," Jeff added, his voice taking on a lighter, more casual tone. "When you're around the other staff, make sure to call me 'Jeff.' I don't want them to know I hired my nephew. Nepotism and all."

"I don't think I've ever called you 'Uncle Jeff,'" Adam muttered, his mind already drifting.

"Huh, yeah, maybe you're right," Jeff said with a chuckle. "Actually, sounds weird coming from you." He slapped Adam on the back, then flicked off the lights in the habitat, leaving them standing in the dim red glow of the exit sign. "You shouldn't have to worry about anything here during any of your shifts. These are the switches for the enclosures, if you need to turn them on or off. In fact, you won't even have a key to this section of the zoo."

Adam nodded, even though his mind was elsewhere. His uncle checked the doors and lights as they walked toward the zoo's main entrance. Adam admired his uncle's attention to detail, envying the way Jeff seemed to care about the small things. But he didn't care about anything anymore. Not really. Especially not the small things.

"You can do good here, Adam," Jeff said, his voice warm but distant. "One day at a time."

"Thanks, Jeff. I really appreciate the chance to work, and the money."

"Anything for Ruby and you," Jeff said, giving him a wink as he headed toward his vehicle.

Adam watched until his uncle's car turned the corner, leaving him alone in quiet darkness. He exhaled a long breath, feeling the weight of the silence. It was always like this now. Alone. The darkness was his refuge, the one place he could breathe. The light, on the other hand, exposed everything he didn't want to remember, everything he couldn't forget.

He grabbed his flashlight, the keys, and the ever-important clipboard, which had a single, almost mocking title on its cover: Monitor, Maintain, and Mind the Grounds: Nightshift at the Prescott, Arizona Zoo.

He started his rounds the way Jeff had shown him, through the reptile pavilion, past the peacocks, and toward the big cats. But when he reached the panther enclosure, he veered east instead of west, slipping away to the bench near the primates. The primate exhibit had cooling misters and a bamboo walkway that obscured him from the security cameras. A moment to hide, to fade into the shadows.

There, Adam threw the clipboard aside, popped in his AirPods, and lit a cigarette. The smoke filled his lungs, its warmth a sharp contrast to the coldness that had settled deep in his chest. He hit play on Coldplay. God, he hated Coldplay. But it wasn't about the music. It wasn't about love or hate, or melody or lyrics. It was about the pain. And Coldplay made it hurt even more.

He scrolled through his phone, but not aimlessly. No, this wasn't about killing time. He wasn't hopping down memory lane. He was going straight for the photo. The one that had burned itself into his mind, like staring at the sun too long. Sometimes guilt only stops gnawing when you let it have a piece of you.

He stared at the photo until it blurred, until the image felt like it was seeping deeper into his soul. But before his cigarette could burn his fingers, a shrill screeching noise sliced through the air behind him, growing louder, wilder, like an orchestra warming up to chaos.

Adam pulled the AirPods from his ears and sat up, heart racing. The sound was alien, something he'd never heard before at the zoo. Panic spiked in his chest. He turned his body toward the chimpanzee enclosure, and his stomach dropped.

The chimps were in full frenzy, clawing at the glass wall at the far end, as if they could climb it, scratching and scraping with frantic desperation. They were trying to escape. No, they were trying to flee, like they were running from something.

Adam put out his cigarette and stood, confusion and fear coiling in his gut like a broken spring. He flipped through the clipboard for answers: feeding schedules, exhibit maps, job descriptions, but there was nothing about erratic animal behavior. Nothing about animals reacting like they were on fucking fire.

Before he could text his uncle, a chill ran down his spine. There, at the far end of the chimp exhibit, silhouetted against the cold fluorescent lights that his uncle made sure to turn off, was Dilly.

The chimpanzee.

The one his uncle had said was sedated. The one who was supposed to be asleep.

But Dilly wasn't asleep.

Dilly was watching him.

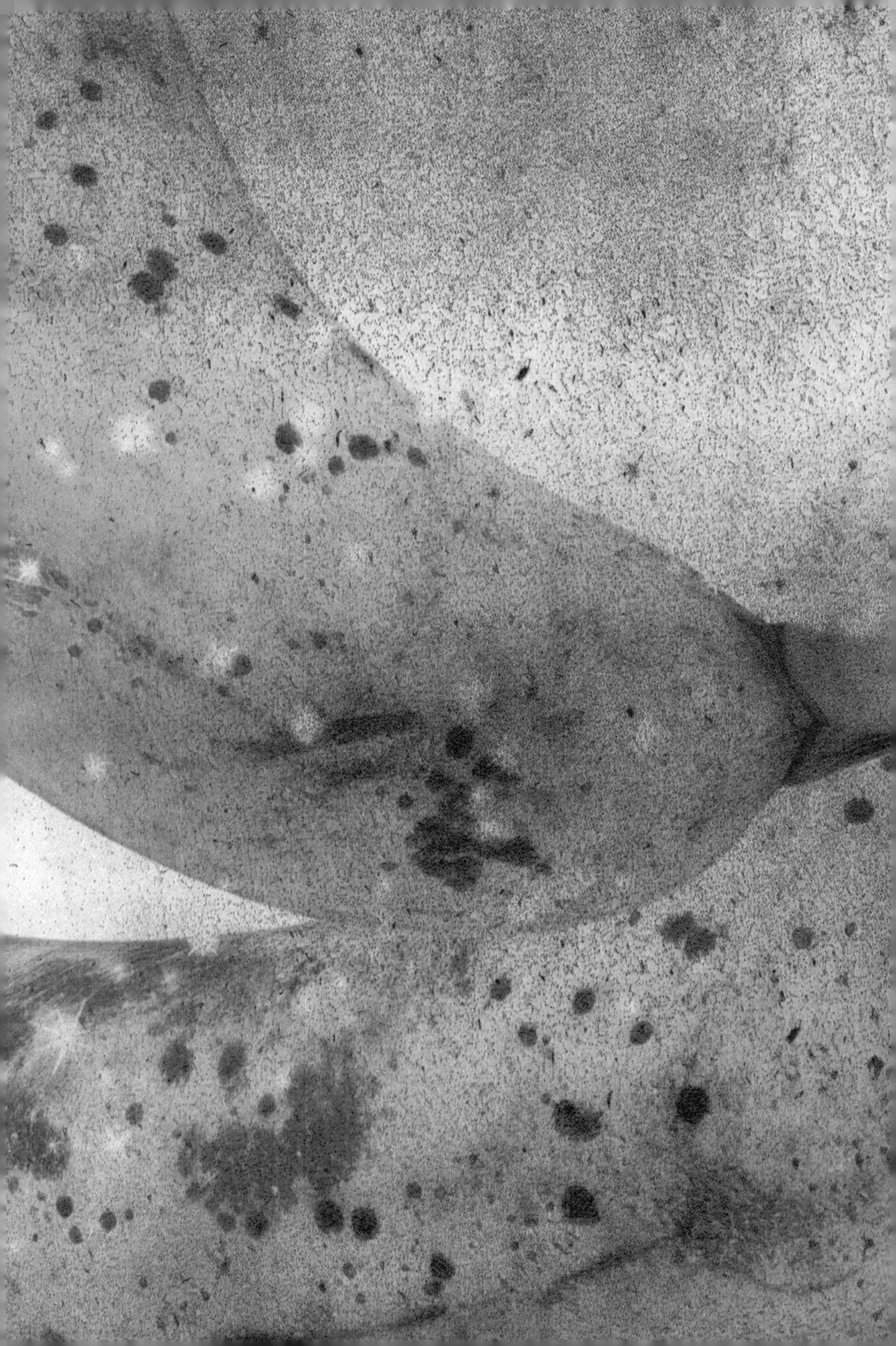

"Now in the morning, I sleep alone."

Coldplay

Chapter 5

Adam unrolled sheets of tin foil in the air, stretching his arms out as if to be crucified. He held the metallic fabric from one end of his window to the other. Then he ripped the sheet and began to tape, position, and dress. He was a seamstress, if only for a minute, creating foil curtains to block the sun. He could already feel the aluminum hot on his fingers as the morning sun cooked it beyond the glass. Slowly, with every tear, the room grew black. Adam hoped that now that he had a nightshift gig, he could finally sleep. He'd learned in mourning that sleep is never the peace it promises; it's a temporary ceasefire between memories too heavy to bear. But a ceasefire is all he wanted. A moment for the bullets to stop.

With the room dark as night, he tossed the left-over foil roll on his desk, piled high with art books, old sketchbooks, and a growing layer of dust. As if his old desires were growing new skin. He hadn't touched a pencil since the accident, and then since he dropped out of liberal arts college. Since then, the only motivation he's had to draw is to draw people out of his life. Drawing lines in the sand felt more satisfying than lead on paper. Adam charged his phone and turned on music while stuffing his head beneath his covers.

Please God, let me sleep, he thought, as he clicked Coldplay on. He popped in his AirPods, rolled over and listened to the weak melodies of lame ass pop music. Every time he hit that triangle play button, he rubbed his eyebrows with the same thought, *God, I hate Coldplay.* He hated them about as much as he hated his existence. *God, I hate myself.* He often thought he'd chew off his own dick to avoid listening to this band. But he couldn't. Not yet anyway. He wanted to sleep, but he needed punishment. Sleep came easier with flagellation than it did with exhaustion. The music, their shitty music, was the form of medieval flogging he needed. As poppy nothingness lyrics squawked in his ear, he could feel his nocturnal mind drifting toward sleep. Hopeful, he tried hard to do nothing and wait. But, as he was crossing the threshold into the unconscious, his younger sister opened the door.

"You awake slut?" she said, kicking the door open. Adam was always bothered by his twelve-year-old sister's foul language, but he had given up on trying to tame her tongue. His make-shift parenting style for raising her had dwindled to just getting out of her way.

From beneath the covers, Adam replied, "Try-ing to be, dildo."

"I wanted to see how your day at work was, Nancy?" she asked with a motherly tone. He hated that she had started speaking like Mom.

"Dude, it was work. It sucked. Get out so I can sleep," Adam said, trying to keep his eyes closed, so as not to miss the Sandman's train.

"Uncle Jeff said you're going to do a fine job," she said, now like their proud father.

"Uncle Jeff is a fucking baked potato," Adam said.

"Ha! What does that mean?" Ruby asked as she leaned against the door frame.

"It means he's hella weird, and brimming with hot nothingness, and he makes me a bit sick."

"Nah, Uncle Jeff is cool. You just don't like him because you think he's trying to be Dad."

"No, he's weird."

"No, you're weird."

"No, he's weird."

"No, *you're* weird."

"Enough!" Adam shouted from bed.

"Well, whatever, I just wanted to tell you . . ." his sister said with a pause. Adam waited, knowing something uncomfortable was about to vomit from her mouth. Something he didn't want to hear, but it was important for her to say, "that you, getting this job to help, and postponing college to be with me--it just means a lot."

"It's fine, you're welcome, Ruby," Adam said, uncovering his face from his blankets, feeling an unease rise inside of him.

"Haha, you're so beta," Ruby said with a snicker.

"Get the fuck out!" Adam said, throwing a pillow at the door, shoving Ruby out and into the hall with her condescending laughter.

"I'm going to the bus stop, see you later, beeotch!" Ruby yelled from the other room, as she slammed the door.

"And it was all yellow"

Coldplay

Chapter 5

Chapter 6

"Who here knows that bananas are cursed?" Emma shouted, pulling a ripe yellow fruit from her canvas bag. She waved it in front of the group, making a dramatic show of it. The kids froze for a moment, and then the debate erupted, a cacophony of shocked exclamations and amused disbelief.

"Cursed? That doesn't make any sense," one of the younger kids called out, his face scrunched up in confusion.

Emma grinned, undeterred. "Oh, you think I'm pulling your chain?" she said, adjusting her safari hat and smoothing down her khaki vest as she straightened to full height. "Well, buckle up, buttercups!"

Adam, leaning against the back fence of the zoo, felt his curiosity spark. He couldn't help but watch the young zookeeper, her eyes glinting with mischief. Part of him was intrigued by the idea of sinister bananas, but mostly he was enchanted by the girl in the safari gear. A few tattoos peeked from beneath the canvas-colored uniform, and they piqued his interest even more.

"When bananas spoil," Emma continued, raising the fruit above her head like a trophy, "they release a hot, poisonous gas into the air. Like a . . . fruit toot." She made a farting noise for effect, causing the kids to burst out laughing. Adam smirked despite himself.

"It's called ethylene," she went on, her voice dropping to a more mysterious tone. "When bananas go bad, they release a colorless, flammable gas that has a sweet taste and smell." She paused for dramatic effect, then reached into her vest pocket and pulled out a lighter.

Adam's heart skipped a beat as he watched her light the spoiled banana. The fruit crackled as it caught fire, the yellow skin curling up around the edges in a burst of bright orange flames. The kids gasped, their laughter faltering into stunned silence. Even Adam took a step back, caught off guard by the sudden explosion of flame.

The flames flickered out almost as quickly as they'd appeared, leaving behind only the charred remnants of the banana.

Emma turned to the crowd with a wicked grin. "When bananas spoil, they can actually be dangerous. Always be careful when something spoils, as whatever's nearby will also spoil. That's why bananas are cursed. It's like the saying, 'one bad apple spoils the bunch.' That's based on the real process of ethylene gas ripening fruit. But when bananas go rotten, you really should be worried. That's when things get—"

"Adam! Over here!" a shout cut through the air. Adam turned to see his Uncle Jeff, waving him over by the zoo office. He felt a pang of disappointment that the moment was over so quickly, but dutifully made his way over.

As Adam walked, he glanced back. To his surprise, Emma caught his eye. She smiled at him, a teasing glint in her gaze, making his heart flutter. Adam felt his face warm, a blush creeping up his neck. He was sure he looked like a fool, caught between excitement and embarrassment. He quickly forced a smile and looked away, hurrying to his uncle.

"I didn't know bananas were cursed," Adam said, a little too loudly, as he reached Jeff.

"Cursed?" Jeff gave him a bemused look, raising an eyebrow. "I wouldn't go that far. But she likes to be dramatic, and the kids like it."

Adam chuckled awkwardly, rubbing the back of his neck. "Yeah, she was just saying something about gases and fruit . . . Has she worked here long?"

Jeff's eyes narrowed with the barest hint of concern. "About a year, why do you ask?"

Before Adam could respond, his uncle snapped his fingers. "Before I forget, I need a favor. A serious favor."

"Uh, sure. What's up?"

"Can you check the timers tonight on the tortoises? Make sure they're still running, and while you're at it, double-check the watering cans." Jeff's tone shifted, his voice growing more serious. "We've been having issues with the filters not kicking on overnight, and needing to be manually turned on after going out."

"Got it."

"We're just trying to stay ahead of it before it becomes a problem," Jeff said, clapping Adam on the back with more force than necessary. "I appreciate you, kid."

Adam flinched at the slap, something tightening in his chest. It wasn't the first time Jeff had done that, and though he'd never say it out loud, Adam hated it. There was something off about the gesture, something off about his uncle. Adam felt he was always trying too hard to assert dominance. But maybe Ruby was right. Maybe Adam just hated men with alpha energy. Still, he couldn't bring himself to protest. He never could.

"Thanks, Jeff. I'll take care of it," Adam said, trying to shake off the discomfort.

But Jeff wasn't done. He called over his shoulder as he started to walk away, his voice carrying with authority. "One more thing! Can I get a key to your place?"

"A key? Like . . . a house key?" Adam blinked, unsure if he'd heard that right. The question, and the sudden seriousness in Jeff's voice, made him pause. It felt . . . odd.

"Yeah, with you and Ruby there, I thought it might be a good idea to have one. You know, just in case you two need anything. Just in case there is an emergency, God forbid."

"Uh, yeah, sure. I'll bring one next time I work," he said, his voice trailing off.

Jeff gave him a final nod, clearly satisfied. "Good. I'll see you tomorrow then. Don't forget!"

"*Everything I know is wrong*
Everything I do, it just comes undone
And everything is torn apart
Oh, and that's the hardest part
That's the hardest part"

Coldplay

Chapter 6

Chapter 7

Adam's phone was hot to the touch, as it had been playing Coldplay for hours. "God, I hate Coldplay," he muttered as he woke from a restless sleep to take a piss. He made his way to the bathroom the way a drunk Spiderman might, stumbling from wall to wall, using his fingers to grip wherever he could. Even though he had to sleep during the day, he wouldn't dare turn on the light, not wanting to fuck up his circadian rhythm, in the hopes that sleep might return to him. But, as he stood there with his dick out, nothing came.

He waited a bit longer . . . no relief.

Now that his mind was fully awake, Adam ventured toward the kitchen to grab whiskey. The last few days he'd started having a few sips here and there. Just to take the edge off. Nothing too serious. He could only afford the cheap shit, Southern Comfort, but remembered back in the day he could steal top-shelf bottles from his dad's cabinet. He poured half a glass into a Muppet mug he'd had since childhood. Drinking straight from the bottle would have felt like admitting he was a drunk, but the mug, bright, silly, familiar, gave him the illusion of satisfied control. A Muppet mug at least made him happy as he tried to erase the unhappiness. Between large gulps, he heard a low, unfamiliar sound behind him in the kitchen, something alive threaded through the mechanical hum of the refrigerator and dishwasher. He quickly turned, a bit spooked, but there was nothing unusual about the room.

Then the sound started again, coming from the fruit bowl on the counter, squelching, like wet flesh being rubbed together. Adam slowly approached the bowl, curious and unsettled all at once.

It was the bananas.

He watched fearfully as the bundle of bananas he purchased two days earlier rolled and squirmed over one another like a snake strangling its prey. He couldn't tell where one banana started and the other ended.

A rush of emotions, disgust, bewilderment, and fear quickly rose, becoming just as tangled up as the satanic fruit he was watching. Adam glanced at the blackened mush in the fruit bowl and shivered. Bananas are cursed. Emma's words rattled through his skull, suddenly less funny and a lot harder to ignore.

But before he could scream or vomit, he heard his sister's voice. "Good morning, schnookums," Ruby sing-songed, handing him a cup of hot coffee. Adam sat straight up, realizing he was sprawled out on the warm kitchen tile, his head pounding with a tight grip on the mug from the night before. The alcohol had dried up, removing the evidence from his younger sister.

"Da fuck you doin' on the floor in the kitchen, Bozo?" Ruby asked as she began pouring a bowl of cereal for dinner.

"What the hell? The bananas, the fucking bananas!" Adam said loudly, hopping to his feet.

"Yeah, let's talk about bananas," Ruby said confidently, leaning up against the kitchen counter.

Adam pulled the bowl close to himself, but was only met with brown mush. As if an ape took a shit into the fruit bowl.

"The hell?" Adam said.

"Whatever you did to my 'nans, now I can't have any with my cereal. Thanks, jackass."

"No, earlier . . . when you were at school," Adam started, voice low, the memory crawling back. Then his eyes met Ruby's. He stopped himself. In that moment, remembering all the shit she'd gone through the last couple of months, the last thing she needed was her last caregiver, her brother, losing his shit about weird fruit. Ruby raised an eyebrow, that signature look that said she wasn't buying the pause.

"Say what?" she asked, eyes sharp, tone flat.

Adam swallowed, forcing a shrug. "I think I sleepwalked. Had a weird dream or something. It's . . . whatever."

Ruby didn't miss a beat. "And pissed all over my 'nans?"

Adam sighed, rubbing his face. "Yeah, maybe. Sure. You ready for school or what?"

"It's evening, cheese brain," Ruby grinned, knowing his new graveyard hours were fucking him up. "But, I do need a ride to Julie's."

"Turn into something beautiful"

Coldplay

Chapter 7

Chapter 8

Adam and Ruby never rode in silence. Ruby always had some new band; some obscure sonic chaos she needed him to hear. Half rebellion, half communion.

"You heard of Battlesnake?" she asked, already swiping open Spotify like a weapon.

"Battlesnake?" Adam raised an eyebrow.

"Well, get ready to have your balls pop," Ruby grinned, jamming the volume up as the car speakers screamed to life with wailing guitars and what she described as "Dragon-Core."

Adam smirked, but his chest was tight. She was deflecting . . . hard. And honestly, he didn't blame her. The evening had been hell for both of them. But guardianship didn't come with eject buttons, and he wasn't going to chicken out. Not this time.

He reached for the knob, turning the music down a few notches. "How are you?" he asked, gently.

"Fine," Ruby said instantly, stabbing the volume back up like a protest.

"No, really." He turned it down again, firmer this time. "How are you, Ruby?"

"I don't get you, dude," Ruby said with frustration. "When I try to talk with you, you get uncomfortable and weird and shit. But when you try to talk to me, I gotta open up and just pretend it's Dr. Phil magic hour. Make up your mind, bro!"

Adam winced. She wasn't wrong, as flashes of his own therapy scraped his brain. "You're right, Ruby," he said, caught like a fly in a web. "I want to be better. I need to be, for you."

"No, dude, for you!" Ruby shouted, facing herself toward the window. "I'm not going to be your messiah or monolith."

"Monolith?" Adam asked, trying to understand.

"Yeah. 2001: A Space Odyssey? Duhhhhh"

"Okay, I still don't get it."

"It's why the monkeys evolved into humans. It launched their . . . You know what? Fuck it." Ruby snapped. "I'm only twelve and I get this. I want us to be good, because we're actually good. I don't want us to pretend we're father and daughter or just going to like, force a smile to try and make this new life work. You need help, Adam. You need to get better, I need to get better, and we need to do it because it's right."

Adam sat in that moment like a man in chains. He had a thousand things he wanted to say, questions, confessions, apologies . . . each of them tasted like gravel in his throat. And Ruby could feel it too. She watched him, waiting. Daring him.

But all he could do was reach for the volume knob again.

The music swelled back.

Coward.

She knew it was his fear and grief fucking each other, making a mutated baby in the form of guilt.

"Fine, have it your way, dickbreath." She stabbed at her phone, killing Battlesnake mid-roar and

replacing it with Coldplay just to throw salt into
Adam's open, leaking wounds.

"Tell me you love me
If you don't, then lie
Oh, lie to me
I wish you'd have let me know
What's really going on below
So much it hurts"

Subject: Urgent Request: Transfer of Last Chimpanzee from our Closing Sanctuary

To Whom It May Concern,

I hope this message finds you well. I am writing to discuss an urgent matter regarding the closing of Chimp Haven, a sanctuary which currently is housing the last living chimpanzee in its care. I received your contact information from our mutual colleague, Megan Claven at ProjectChimp.

As you may have heard, our beloved sanctuary is unfortunately closing down, and we are reaching out to respected institutions like yours to consider providing a new home for our last chimpanzee, Daffodil. Given Prescott AZ Zoo's reputation for excellence in animal care and conservation efforts, we believe your facility would be an ideal environment for the chimpanzee to thrive and receive the best possible care.

We understand that decisions of this nature require careful consideration, and we are prepared to assist in any way we can to facilitate a smooth transition. Our team is ready to discuss logistics, including transportation and any necessary paperwork, to ensure that the transfer process is seamless.

Please let us know at your earliest convenience if P.A.Z. would be willing to accommodate Daffodil. We are committed to working closely with you to ensure the well-being of this animal. Daffodil is special and has overcome many obstacles to get where he is today.

Thank you for considering this request. I look forward to your response.

Warm regards,
Bryan Teegan

*"When you're feeling low, and your resistance is low
Light another cigarette and let yourself go."*

Coldplay

Chapter 8

Chapter 9

Adam pulled into the zoo's entrance, greeted by the cheerful painted signs of cartoon zebras and lions smiling about their imprisonment. He wished he could fake it as well as they could.

As he exited his car, he tapped his shirt pocket to make sure his cigarettes were where they were supposed to be, then poured the rest of his Jim Beam into his gas station fountain drink. He gave one more exhale before walking toward the zoo's entrance, bracing himself for another long night of nothingness.

His uncle didn't work on Thursdays, making today a bit of a relief. Adam wouldn't have to pretend he was stoked about the job or navigate small talk. Upon entering the zoo office, he gave a nod to the receptionist, who also doubled as a caretaker, and snagged his lanyard, keys, torch, and clipboard.

He was halfway out the door when a question seized him in his tracks.

"Bananas, huh?" Emma asked as she came around the corner, getting ready to head out for the day.

Adam's blood turned to concrete, forcing him to stop dead.

"What did you say?" turning to face her.

"Bananas. Jeff said you were interested in my talk about bananas?"

Adam could feel the concrete breaking apart in his veins, allowing him to relax.

"You're the new night shift guy, right?" Emma asked, putting her hand out for a shake.

"Yeah, my name is Adam."

"Emma."

For the first time, he saw her. Really saw her. His eyes tracked the dimples blooming and fading on her cheeks like tiny eclipses, freckles scattered across her nose like cosmic constellations. He wanted to trace every one of them with his finger-tip, just to see if she'd laugh or pull away.

But he didn't. He couldn't. He wiped his sweaty palms against his jeans, caught between nerves and instinct, and offered her a firm handshake instead.

"I didn't know bananas were cursed," he said, trying not to sound like a fool, clipboard tucked under his arm like armor. "That's cool."

She smiled at him again, brighter this time, and he wondered if this was how it started for normal people? Not with fireworks, but with freckles and a stupid fruit story they'd never forget.

"They're not really," she said with a sideways smile. "They're just natural sources of ethylene, which include both natural gas and petroleum. It's a naturally occurring hormone in plants that inhibits growth and promotes leaf fall. And in fruits, promotes ripening. So, it's more science than it is supernatural." Adam ricocheted the smile, raising a brow. "Jesus, that's a lot." "It's more fun for the kids if it's supernatural instead of science."

"Wait," Adam blurted, his curiosity pulling him back to the night before, "so are bananas okay to eat if they're spoiled or too ripe?"

"Yeah, dude, you're fine. That actually makes the best banana bread," she said, punching her timecard.

"And can they rot . . . like, super-fast?"

"Sure, in heat or the right setting, I guess?" Adam nodded, trying to line up her answers with what he'd seen previously. "You really like bananas, huh?" Emma asked, brow furrowing with curiosity.

"Uh, sure. Yeah," Adam said, then immediately hated everything about himself.

"I bet you do, "she said with a wink.

Oh my god, was she actually flirting with me? He froze for a beat, then blurted the first thing that came to mind. "Well, not in that way," he said, worried she was thinking something he didn't want her to think."What way?" she asked, tilting her head, teasingly challenging him to explain.

" . . ."

"Look at us, a couple of monkeys liking bananas," Adam said, attempting to flirt and dodge, but failing in the process.

"Yeah, I guess so. But monkeys can't really have bananas. Well, not the ones at the grocery store anyway. Too much sugar. Not good for their diet," Emma said, matter-of-factly.

"Oh, right, Jeff told me that. I was speaking more . . . theoretically. *Idiot. Now I look like I sit around theorizing about monkeys and bananas. Any*ways, I'd better hit my rounds."

"Bye, banana boy."

"Bye . . . banana girl?" He gave a two-finger salute to his forehead and made his way to the door.

Ruby's right. I am a cockface, beta.

The summer sunset was dragonfruit pink, blending into purple, with a few stars breaking through. For a moment, Adam was stunned by the Arizona beauty, but then he put his eyes toward the ground and began his trail. He often didn't allow himself the appreciation of life, knowing it would be sucked out of him by the fangs of god.

One round per hour is spent here; the rest of the time is spent watching the monitors and habitat levels from the control room that everyone here calls "The Crow's Nest."

Every animal has limited water amounts, nutrient quantities, and even timed light and heating periods. His job wasn't to mess with any of it, just making sure the machines were doing their jobs. Now, being here multiple nights in a row, Adam had made the firm decision that this job was creepy as fuck. An unease was settling in for him, because even though you couldn't see anything beyond your flashlight in the late hours, there was a sense of being watched, which is perfectly valid, because you were being watched. The zoo came alive at night in ways it would never in the heat of the Arizona sun. Noises unnatural to man stung the air, making Adam turn his head with every croak and cry.

Beyond just the enclosed animals, a circus of critters came from beneath the zoo to eat trash and fuck. Adam's growing insomnia wasn't a disease; it was natural. Here he was, a nocturnal with the nocturnals. After a round or two, Adam needed a cigarette. Truthfully, he always needed a cigarette. He grabbed his midnight lunch and made way toward his private, misty haven, the chimpanzee enclosure. There, Adam lit his addiction and plopped on the bench with his back against the chain-link. He opened his phone, his mind no longer needed to instruct his thumbs where to go. They knew exactly where the secrets lay, like trained, hairless rats. Adam stared at the selfie of his parents, each of them in teal and purple Arizona Diamondback hats, heading to the game. His mind was like going through a file folder, pulling out every case file from that moment. The smell of the car's leather, how the vehicle's AC battled against the Phoenix sun, how his father air drummed to Coldplay's Viva La Vida. Adam's eyes began to mist, fog rolling in from somewhere deep inside him, clouding the edges of his vision. Guilt, grief, or exhaustion, he could no longer tell the difference. But before he could groan or blink it away, something tapped him on the shoulder.

Not a breeze, or a leaf. A deliberate touch. He froze, as somewhere in the dark behind him, something was trying to get his attention. An extraterrestrial making contact with humanity. Then came the jolt. A hand, paw, or claw brushing against skin, and breaking the fragile calm of the night.

"Cocksucker!" Adam shouted, stumbling forward from the fence in a burst of panic. He slipped on the loose gravel, his lunch and clipboard launching from his grip and crashing against the hard, uneven stone. He cursed under his breath, hating himself for letting his guard down. Of course, the animals could reach through. He knew that he should have remembered that. As he scrambled to his feet, heart hammering, he turned toward the fence and saw it.

Daffodil.

The chimp stood upright, two legs planted like a man's, arms low and calm at his sides. He didn't twitch. He didn't blink. He just stood there in the dark, like he'd been waiting.

How long has Dilly been there, watching me? Adam thought, birthing fear.

The low zoo lights cast just enough of a glow to ignite those awful yellow eyes, burning through the night like furnace coals. Adam couldn't move. For a moment, neither could Dilly. Their stares locked, a pulse of something supernatural moving between them, like recognition or a shared wound. Adam's chest rose and fell like crashing waves, but his breath began to slow. He bent down slowly, eyes never leaving the mass of shadow beyond the chain-link.

"Good monkey," Adam whispered, reaching for the scattered remains of his lunch and clipboard.

Daffodil didn't move. He didn't nod. He didn't blink. He just stood there. Watching.

Once Adam realized the monkey wasn't making any sudden movements, he could feel his muscles begin to relax. It was then that Adam noticed what Ruby packed him for lunch: a frozen burrito in a

Ziploc and a mushy banana, which she had written in pen on its browning peel, "a dick for a dickhead" with a smiley face. For half a second, Adam swore he smelled it again, the sickly-sweet rot from the night before, the sound of slick flesh twisting in the fruit bowl.

Dilly's finger came up with a curl, pointing at the banana. Adam's entire experience from the night before was pulsing through the crevices of his brain. *Do I hand it over? What if he grabs me instead? Emma's voice cut through his brain: Bananas are cursed . . . too much sugar. Not good for their diet.*

Adam hesitated, the memory of her teasing grin crashing into the yellow-eyed stare in front of him.

He put the cigarette in his mouth and took a deep drag, as if his brain needed the nicotine fuel to make the right decision. Then, with zero fucks given, he slowly handed the banana to the chimpanzee. Dilly reached out with eerie grace, fingers curling around the fruit with a tenderness that was too clean, too rehearsed. Every movement was precise, almost surgical, like he had done this before, like he was following a script only he understood. There was no twitch, no grunt, no sign of primal impulse. This wasn't instinct; it was intention. Why did nothing about this creature feel like an animal?

"There you go, dude," Adam whispered, sitting down next to the fence. "Be careful though, monkey, apparently bananas are fucking flammable," he said with a snort.

After watching Adam sit down, Dilly followed suit on the other end of the fence. Adam just watched, almost enjoying himself in the wildness of the moment. He lit another cigarette, as Dilly unwrapped his mushy fruit. But then, Adam watched Dilly do something he'd never expected. Dilly pretended the banana was a cigarette. Adam would raise a hand; Dilly would raise a hand. Adam would flip a bird; Dilly would return it. Adam grunted, Dilly grunted. The two of them mirrored each other, clones of the other, devilish doppelgangers. Adam watched the monkey watching him. He couldn't explain it, but he felt that Dilly was aware. Not just aware of his surroundings, like every other conscious animal. Adam felt unease as if the beast knew more than any beast should, as if he could smell Adam's secrets in the hot air. But, as Adam reached for his phone to record the moment, he realized the last picture of him and his parents sat there, glowing like blue fire. Dilly's eyes left Adam's and focused his concentration on the phone. On the photo.

Adam's discomfort grew at the idea of a conscious creature seeing that photo as he quickly clicked the phone black, his thoughts swirling at the absurdity of a monkey judging him. Then the chimpanzee did something unexpected.

It grinned.

It nodded as if agreeing with his thoughts.

"When you try your best, but you don't succeed
When you get what you want, but not what you need
When you feel so tired, but you can't sleep
Stuck in reverse"

Coldplay

Adam's phone rang just as his mind was beginning to slip into sweet, unconscious oblivion within the dark void of his room, the words "Jeff Potato" flashed on the phone's screen, momentarily blinding him.

"Hey Jeff," Adam said in a slumberer's tone.

"Adam, what the fuck?!" His uncle had his full attention, as Adam sat up quickly in bed. "What? What happened?!"

"Did you check the timers for the tortoises like I told you to?" Adam's mind burst with every curse word in the sailor's dictionary.

"Um, yes? Shit, sorry, I think I did." Silence on the other end of the line increased Adam's fear of the repercussions. "Is everything alright?"

"No, Adam. Everything is not alright. We lost all of the tortoises."

"What? You lost them?"

"Dead, jackass!" his uncle said, snapping at the sleepless boy.

"Wait, because their water dispenser timers weren't checked?"

"Well, that's what we're trying to figure out. The timers stopped working around the middle of your shift. When we came in this morning, they were dried up like dog shit in the sun. And now three tortoises, each over a hundred years old, are dead in their fucking habitat."

"Fuck me. I'm so sorry, but I–"

"When you get here tonight, we'll discuss it more."

"Fine, yeah, of course, sounds good," Adam said, rubbing the back of his neck. The heat steaming from his skin could fry an egg.

"Just tell me this, were you just not doing your rounds and fucking off? Or were you drinking again?"

The question felt like medieval torture, pulling his limbs apart with chains and hooks.

"Jeff, not at all, I mean, no . . . I did my rounds, but I got a bit distracted with Daffodil."

"Daffodil?" his uncle said with a confused tenor.

"Yeah, I was, well, I guess hanging with him. He was interacting with me and–"

"Were you in the medical enclosure?" his uncle said, interrupting him.

"No, just at the guest entrance of the chimpanzee enclosure."

"What are you talking about, Adam?! Daffodil hasn't been released from the medical facility yet, where you and I left him."

Adam's mind turned to mush as it tried to put the pieces back together from the night before. Wait. If he wasn't released . . . then who the hell was I with? The memory slammed into him, the slick noise of bananas twisting in the dark, the smell of rot clinging to the air, and those yellow eyes burning like lanterns in the dark. "Wait, what? What do you mean?"

"We'll discuss it when you get here this evening. I'm not happy with you Adam," Jeff said, hanging up on him.

"Wait, Jeff, Daffodil wasn't out last night?!"

Chapter 11

Emma sang loudly in the shower. Well, truthfully, she sang loudly everywhere. Her shower just had better acoustics. She knew she didn't have a pair of pipes in her, but she had the soul of a diva or siren. She didn't give two shits about shaving her legs, not seeing the point, as she breathed her shower cigarette between botched lyrics of Coldplay's High Speed.

Can anybody fly this thing?
Before my head explodes,
Or my head starts to ring.
We've been living life inside a bubble,
We've been living life inside a bubble.

She'd run out of shampoo weeks ago and had been using dish soap to get the job done. *If it can clean pizza grease out of a pan, it can wash grease out of hair*, she thought. She heard the beeping of her phone, pulled it into the shower, and saw that the zoo was requesting her to come in earlier for her shift. *Shit*, she thought as she worked to get the remaining dish soap out of her hair. Her stomach clenched. Earlier shifts usually meant trouble.

Emma has lived by herself since the divorce, confident that marriage for her would never happen again. Her apartment was about as neat as the back rooms of the zoo, but that was the point. She'd always felt feral in the human world, preferring to live more wild than other women. When she was younger, she resonated with Eve in the garden, who preferred the company of snakes to naked idiots. Her apartment was filled with books, old fast-food garbage that operated as ashtrays, and thrift store vinyls. The more albums she could find of someone she'd never heard of, the happier she'd be.

She was a creature of discovery, always prowling for something to satisfy her cat-like curiosity. Upon her walls hung yellow post-it notes filled with random gibberish, from puns to ideas for novels she'd never write. Emma loved ideas but hated execution. Her father used to always say she'd be "president one day. President of ProcrastiNATION." She just realized one day she'd never had a need for anything from anyone. Her happiness was found not in achievement, but in attitude. She prided herself on always being in control, even when it looked like her life was a wildfire of chaos; chaos received like a gift.

Emma grabbed her safari uniform from beneath a KFC bucket, smelt the pits for that formidable smell of onions, shrugged, and threw it on. She sprayed herself down with Walgreens Pharmacy cologne for men that she found in the lost and found at work, grabbed a handful of cheese sticks, and smashed them into her tote.

She unwrapped another and tossed it into the open terrarium on her kitchen island. There, beneath a blue, fluorescent bulb, lived her goliath-bird-eater tarantula, Munchkin. A year ago, she had stolen the spider from the zoo, claiming it had escaped. She couldn't sit with the fact that the spider's enclosure was the size of a toaster.

Ever since then, Munchkin had been the man she'd come home to. She often would joke with the spider that he was the perfect man for her: a good provider, built his own home, hairy as a lumberjack, good teeth, and multiple arms for lovemaking. Munchkin's terrarium was also far too small for his size, and it didn't help that she had a small disco ball and a He-Man action figure imprisoned in there with the arachnid. So often, she'd just leave the lid off, allowing the creature to roam at its leisure in the apartment. Typically, Munchkin watched Emma as if she were a fly, bouncing from place to place as she usually did. But this time, Munchkin was watching something else.

There, sitting on Emma's counter, was a bundle of bananas. The spider perched itself upon the fruit as if it were a nest. The striking, yellow color hit Emma like a stoplight, invoking a smile as she thought about Adam at the zoo. After nudging Munchkin over, she ripped one off and threw it into her canvas tote as a gesture, a flirt, for the quiet nightshift boy who's way too interested in bananas.

"Bye, Munch!" she called out, walking toward the front door. And like that, Emma was out the door. Leaving her shit hole unlocked as usual. But, beneath the Christmas lights that dangled in her kitchen, something supernatural touched down upon her home. An incarnation from another world, as the ripe banana bunch began to mold and rot at a rate not seen in nature. The yellow fruit percolated to a frothy, black bubble. Sludge like magma leaked down the sides of the counter and onto the dirty floor. Munchkin quickly moved off the counter. The banana bundle twisted and turned like worms in fire, pulsing with breath and mushy blood. Becoming more than bananas.

Subject: Urgent Request: Transfer of Last Chimpanzee from Closing Sanctuary

Dear Director Teegan,

Thank you for reaching out to us regarding Daffodil. We are saddened to hear that the sanctuary is closing, and appreciate the trust you have placed in The Prescott Zoo as a potential new home for this special animal. May I ask what has happened? I've tried to discover what I could online but could not discern any reasoning as to why Chimp Haven is closing and you're needing to re-home all the chimpanzees.

Nonetheless, after careful consideration and review of our current capacities and commitments, we regret to inform you that we are unable to accommodate the chimpanzee at this time. This decision was not made lightly, and we understand the importance of finding a suitable and caring environment for the chimpanzee's future. Let us know if we can accommodate by offering our own references and recommendations.

We commend your efforts in ensuring the well-being of this chimpanzee and wish you the best in finding a suitable alternative. If there are any changes in circumstances or if there are other ways we can assist in the future, please do not hesitate to reach out.

Thank you once again for considering P.A.Z. We appreciate your understanding.

Best regards,
Jeffrey Harrison Director | Prescott AZ Zoo

*"So I look in your direction
But you pay me no attention do you
I know you don't listen to me
Cause you say you see straight through me don't you"*

Coldplay

Chapter 11

Chapter 12

Adam left early for work, determined to find answers, or at least proof that the chimp had actually gotten out before he had to face his uncle.

In the kitchen, he grabbed a Ziploc bag and stuffed it with a few slices of bread, then took an entire jar of peanut butter from the pantry. He reached for a banana from the fruit bowl, a bundle Ruby had picked up the day before on her way home from school. But after a moment of holding it, turning it over in his hand, he tossed it back into the bowl as if it had whispered something to him. His stomach knew he wasn't ready for that one. Not yet.

There wasn't time to hesitate. He had a major screwup to confront on the other side of town, and his only hope was to get to the zoo early enough to check the security footage from the chimp enclosure. If he could just find one frame of Dilly's escape, maybe he could piece the madness together.

As Adam reached for the car keys on the counter, his eyes caught something that didn't belong. A pack of toothpicks, neatly placed beside the bowl of keys and wallets. Something about it made his gut go cold. *Had Jeff been here without him knowing?* Not wanting to waste another second, Adam bolted out the door and headed straight for the zoo. He wouldn't admit it out loud, but the urgency gave him something to hold onto. The drive, the mission, the sense of movement, it felt good, like a breath of life for a soul running on fumes.

Slipping in through the back entrance and avoiding the other employees, Adam moved quickly and quietly toward the security office. Once inside, he pulled up the surveillance footage and rewound to the moment he had stepped away for lunch the night before, his eyes locked on the timestamp in the corner of the screen. As the footage played, his breath hitched, as if his lungs forgot what to do.

"There is no way," he whispered into the dark, the red server lights blinking around him like quiet alarms, pulsing with every second that passed.

Adam watched the footage in stunned silence as the screen showed him entering the chimp enclosure at 11:14 p.m. and not emerging until 6:00 a.m., walking straight to his car and driving off to end his shift.

"Not possible," he muttered. "Just not fucking possible," he said louder, pushing his chair back from the desk. *I remember doing multiple rounds. I remember every step, opening gates, checking rooms. It's just not fucking possible.* His thoughts darted like serpents, fast and biting, each one trying to take a piece of what he believed was real.

"Hey! There you are!" Emma said brightly, flicking on the lights. "Geez, you look like horse shit. You okay?" she asked, coming around the desk.

Adam quickly slammed the laptop and swung his chair around. "I'm fine, what's up?" he could feel his face wasn't matching up with his words, and giving away that everything was definitely not alright.

"Well, okay," Emma replied trepidatiously, "Jeff is looking for everyone, we're all gonna meet at the tortoise habitat."

"Right, got it. Thanks."

"Oh! I brought you something," Emma said, smiling reaching into her tote she had slung around her shoulder. She removed a banana and giggled. "Sorry, I couldn't help myself."

Adam stared at it, not laughing, but bothered.

Bothered more now than before. At its goblin yellow flesh. At the brown mold growing like rot under its skin. And its dick-like stem is pointing right at his face.

"Jesus, you're a weird dude. I like it," Emma said, taking it back. Adam quickly realized he was losing it and forced a laugh.

"You're hilarious. Thanks, I'll take it," he said, forcing the glazed look over his eyes away as he shoved it into his vest pocket. Emma just watched the awkward nightshift boy but decided to give up and abandoned him with his banana.

"Whatever, later dude," she said with a confident laugh, to which Adam replied with, "Later dude," very much unconfidently.

Adam turned around to click off the rest of the monitors that were on, but not without first laying eyes on Dilly.

Dilly, through the grainy screen, was staring at the camera in the medical facility where his uncle said he was. Through the noisy resolution, Adam could tell he was smiling at the camera, at him, through him. Adam kept watching the primate's fucking face as his finger reached for the power button. Two primates connected through a static portal. Adam felt a plop by his shoe and noticed that his other hand had squeezed the banana, where ooze ejaculated between the crevices of his fingers, streaking the tile in a sickly, yellow smear, that mirrored the waste of his life.

The air felt heavier with each step as Adam appr-oached the closed-off tortoise enclosure. Most of the staff had gathered, their faces blank or blistered with anger, listening as Jeff addressed them in low, strained tones. His voice carried across the sand like a funeral bell, detailing what had happened and what would happen next.

In the center of the habitat, surrounded by zoo decorations and that distinct Arizona red clay dirt, lay three giant tortoise bodies, unmoving and gro-tesquely still. Their shells were cracked and looked like broken coffins; the homes they've carried their whole lives now becoming their caskets.

Adam froze.

He couldn't look at the bodies too long.

He couldn't stop looking either.

The silence around him was pierced only by the sound of someone stifling a sob.

He scanned the faces. None looked at him. And yet he felt seen in the worst way.

Judged. Or maybe it was just the guilt leaking out of his pores like oil. That sticky kind of shame that clings to you, no matter how many times you try to explain it away. A feeling he's grown so familiar with, it was no different than a new appendage.

Emma stood near his uncle at the far end, arms crossed, lips tight, trying to absorb every word.

Some employees wept.

Others fired questions like accusations.

Adam said nothing.

The banana boy had no words left to offer, only the gnawing ache that somehow, again, something had died under his watch.

"What we know as of now is that the timer's failed," Jeff said to the crowd.

"But that doesn't make any sense as to why all three of them died," one caretaker shouted from the back.

"Have we checked the cameras?" another shouted.

"We have, and unfortunately, it was too dark to really get a good grasp of the situation," Jeff said with disappointment, twirling the toothpick in his mouth. "What we do know is we're getting new timers installed today and reassuring this will never happen again."

"How can you promise that?" a question from one of the reptile keepers.

"Because we're putting all the proper procedures in place. Plans have been discerned, and we're doing the best we can, with the best systems in place. What we don't need at this time, Craig, is pessimism, but earnestness."

As Adam listened to his uncle fight for what easily could be his fault entirely, his eyes slipped to Emma, who stood behind Jeff. She was distracted by something near her, the bushes by her feet.

Adam watched as Emma kicked some of the brush, moved a rock or two with her feet, and then reached down and picked up a banana peel. From his distance, Adam could see a yellow brown skin flap pinched between her fingers as she turned it over in her hands like a miner's diamond. Then Adam saw something he never expected, some unreadable writing and a doodled smiley face his sister had graffitied upon it. *It can't be*, he thought to himself, *it fucking can't be.*

Then, Emma looked up from the disregarded banana peel, right at Adam.

"Some catapult had fired you.
You wonder if your chance'll ever come.
Or if you're stuck in square one"

Coldplay

Chapter 12

Chapter 13

The zoo had been closed all day due to the incident, which they were spinning to the public as *"Closed for Routine Staff Training."* There, Jeff sat on the sand, watching the flies dancing upon the departed. His teeth chewed the toothpick in his mouth, squeezing his saliva from the wood. The harder he thought, the harder he bit. He knew what he had to do, but couldn't bring himself to make the decision.

As he was picking himself up, he noticed something odd about the dead turtle. It seemed as if the turtle's eye was twitching beneath its closed leathery eyelid.

Jeff, with a sense of hopefulness, took out a pen from his pocket, using it to lift the reptile's eyelid. The discharge from the eye had worked like glue and sealed the lids shut, forcing Jeff to work harder in separating the flaps. After a moment, he was able to penetrate it and lift, revealing the cause of the twitch.

The eyes were mush. Pale, yellow, mush like that of banana meat. The smell hit him next, sour and cloying, the same smell that had been crawling through Adam's nightmares. The spheres looked more like balls of spoil, oozing outward. Jeff grabbed his phone and searched the internet for answers and clues. Finding nothing, he resorted to filming the eye with one hand as his other pulled apart the eyelid skin.

"Jesus, what the hell is going on?" Jeff whispered to himself. But he quickly stopped as he heard Adam talking in the distance.

"Tonight's going to be your last night for a while," Jeff said sternly, leading Adam through the zoo office. Adam hadn't been spoken to with such authority in some time. That fatherly tone aroused parts of him that he thought died with his parents. He hated that he craved it.

"Wait, for real, Jeff?" Adam said, coming to terms with the implications of this decision.

"Listen, Adam, it's not a firing, but a suspension."

"Fuck."

"Fuck indeed. But if we figure out what's going on sooner, and it doesn't reveal any negligence on your part. Then we'll have you back immediately. I promise," his uncle said, putting his hand on Adam's arm. "But this will at least protect both of us for a little bit until things get situated."

"Wait, what if it *is* negligence? And I just messed up?"

"Then we'll figure that out when it comes up."

"If it comes up," Adam said, correcting his uncle.

"If. Right," Jeff said, his tone softening, as if remembering he was still the boy's uncle.

"Uncle Jeff, I need this job, or the court won't rule Ruby to be able to stay with me before the next hearing."

"I understand, but my hands are tied. Plus, if that happens, she'll always have a place to stay with me."

"She?"

"Well, you're an adult. You'll be heading back to school."

Adam rubbed his eyes raw at the thought of his world continuing to unravel. "Wait, Jeff, you know I didn't like, kill those turtles, right?"

"Tortoises," his uncle said, interrupting him.

"Sorry, tortoises. There is no way forgetting their timer would have done this. How's it possible that they all die the same night, at the same time?"

The question arrested Jeff for a moment, "That's what we'll figure out."

"Jesus, I mean, how is this my fault?" Adam asked, knowing he shouldn't have.

"You want some tough love, Adam?"

"Not really."

"Well, too bad. Adam, you need to grow up," Jeff said with that fatherly disposition, stiffening his back and stepping closer to his nephew. "I know you're in pain, but your carelessness is now introducing more pain to yourself and those around you. I mean, shit, you're the one who wanted to be a caretaker for Ruby, so take care of her. Your parents wouldn't want this for you. For God's sake, they'd be embarrassed to see you right now." Adam's eyes wanted to stay locked to his uncles, the way a dog would in a fight. But they broke and hit the floor. Jeff could feel he'd said too much and flicked off the office lights.

"We'll talk more about it later. Today's the end of the pay period, so here's your check. Finish tonight's rounds, and then we'll reconvene in a week or so, okay?" he said, patting his nephew's shoulders. Hastily, Jeff shut and locked the office door and walked to the entrance gate. Adam just watched the way he did on his first day, only a week ago, and now again on his last day.

Did he care about this job?

Not even a little fucking bit.

Did Adam care about his sister and their imminent financial needs? Absolutely. He reached into his pocket, pulled out a cigarette, and thought, *fuck it*, as he walked to the chimpanzee enclosure for a premature break.

Subject: Urgent Request: Transfer of Last Chimpanzee from Closing Sanctuary

Jeffrey,

My name is Nancy. I was Mr. Teegan's assistant here for the last handful of years at Chimp Haven.

I'm stepping in with correspondence as unfortunately, I must share with you some deeply saddening news. Bryan Teegan, who you had previously communicated with, has recently passed away due to a tragic accident. His loss has been a profound shock to all of us here, and we are navigating this difficult time with heavy hearts.

Mr. Teegan was deeply passionate about animal welfare and primate conservation, and he would have wanted to see every last chimpanzee receive the best possible care. In his memory and honor, the zoo board has decided to reconsider our initial offer.

We understand the urgency of the situation and are willing to offer significant financial support to facilitate the transfer and provide ongoing care for the chimpanzee.

Please let us know if this revised offer aligns with your current needs and if we can proceed with making arrangements.

Thank you for your consideration during this challenging time.

Nancy Hesson

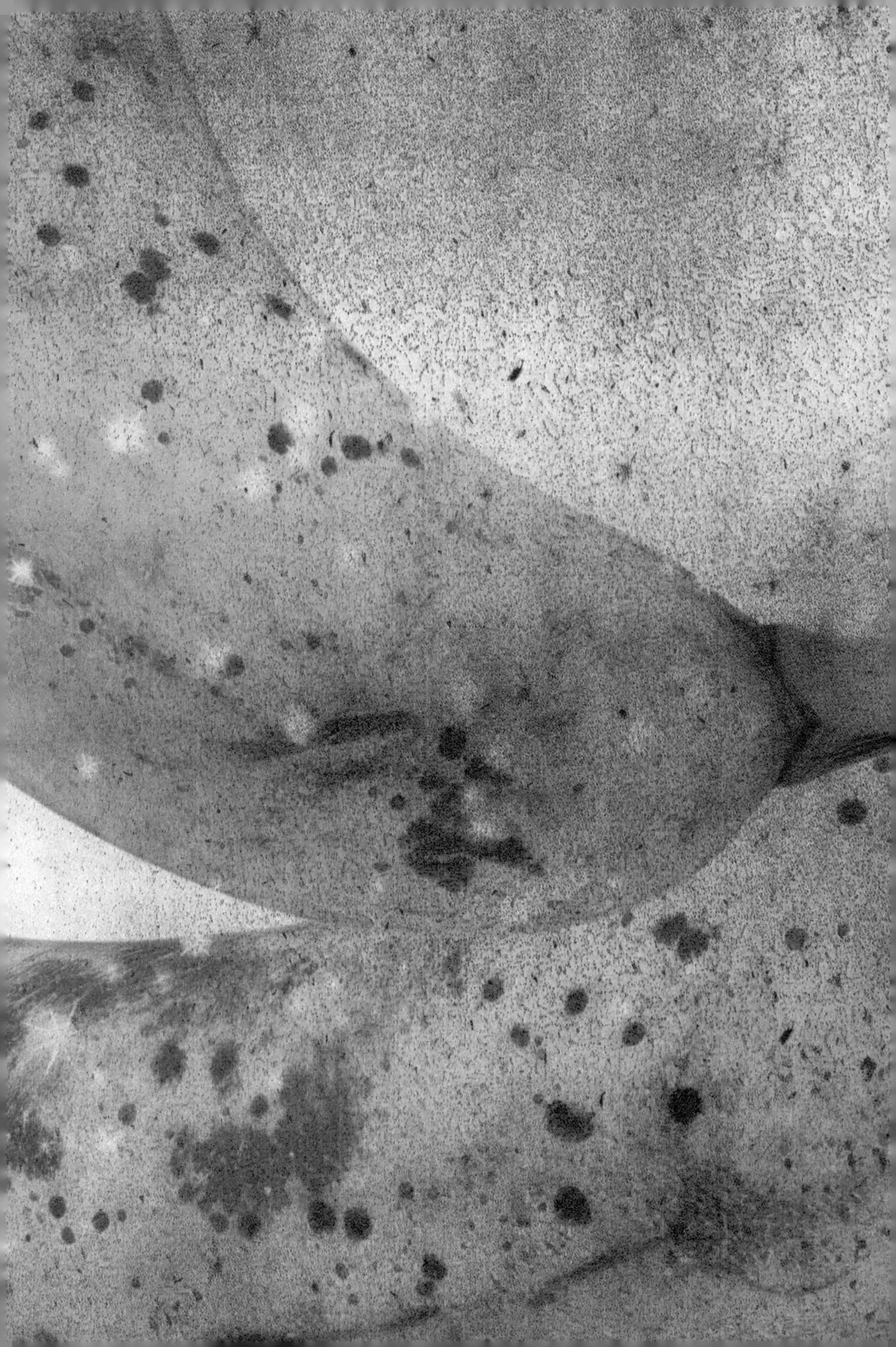

"Give me real, don't give me fake
Open up your eyes"

Coldplay

Chapter 13

Chapter 14

Adam waited, fixing his eyes on the black jungle beyond the chain-link fence. He reasoned that if he wasn't going to be around for a while, he might as well see what the fuck was up with this monkey. But the longer he waited, the more he realized it was pointless. He could see the other chimpanzees in the distance in their makeshift tire and plastic stick treehouse, sleeping and picking at each other's flesh. No sign of Dilly.

Of course, motherfucker, Adam thought to himself between drags. *When I look for you, you don't show*. The entire zoo felt like a pet cemetery, with no sign of anything remotely suspicious or curious. The lack of events left room for his mind to fill with condemnation and blame the chimp for his own sleepless insanity. Adam sobered up, finished his cigarette, and flicked it into the bushes as he made his way back to the security office to view the monitors and finish his final night.

As he walked back, he realized that the zoo was eerily quiet, as if the animals had forgotten their ways.

As if they forgot they were animals.

As if the moon was gone.

He poured himself a shitty cup of coffee and snuck into his uncle's office knowing exactly where he kept the cheap-ass bourbon. A heavy pour into the black coffee, a swig, a pour, and another swig. Soon, Adam was drinking straight from the bottle. At the security desk, Adam pulled his phone from the pocket of his staff vest and popped in his Air-Pods. He tapped the play button. Coldplay filled his ears, and he immediately rolled his eyes. *God, I hate Coldplay*, he thought.

He flipped the monitor over to the chimpanzee medical habitat. "Where are you, ya bitch?" he muttered, the alcohol hot in his system. A single belch could have sparked a fireball. His eyes locked on the glowing screen. If he had the keys, he would've gone in himself, but his access to the veterinary wing was almost nonexistent.

So he sat there, simmering, watching, letting his buzz blur the edge of everything.

But what he saw filled him with dread.

Just as he predicted, Dilly wasn't where he should be.

Adam hurried the best he could to rewind all of the cameras at the zoo, feeling a drunken sense of purpose, a sense of retribution. He wasn't sure how he'd prove it, but he felt the monkey had some hand in the deaths of the turtles, how else would that banana peel have ended up there. Chris Martin's voice rang out:

> *Late night watching TV*
> *Used to be you here beside me*
> *Is there someone there to reach me*
> *Or someone there to find me*

Every feed came back empty and filled with noisy darkness. Adam clicked to the next feed, the next feed, the next feed, the next feed. Then he found him, the chimpanzee was there in the middle of the screen, liberated from his habitat and loose in the zoo. Adam zoomed in to see that the monkey was just standing still, peering into a window. Adam pushed in more; he felt like a military drone officer zeroing in on his target. "Got you, ya lil' bitch." But then, Adam saw it.

Dilly wasn't looking into just any window. He was staring directly into the security office window, the one where Adam now sat. Adam froze. Slowly, he removed the AirPods from his ears and turned toward the window. Yellow eyes were already there, watching him. His chair screeched backward as he jolted in fear, knocking over his bourbon. The liquor splashed across the laptop keyboard in a messy arc, sizzling slightly as it soaked into the electronics.

Adam knew what he had to do and shot up to run outside to film the escaped chimp. "I got you now . . . you, King Kong fuck!" Adam darted like an arrow to the security office door, Dilly waiting for him on the other side. The chimpanzee ran on all fours from the nightshift boy, forcing him to open his camera's phone and follow in pursuit. "Stop, bitch!" he yelled as the chimpanzee made his way through the zoo's pathways, slowly at times, making sure Adam was still on his trail, even waiting for him to catch up before it took off again.

It finally arrived at the chimpanzee enclosure, to the corner where the cameras didn't reach. A small territory of jungle in the heart of the Arizona desert. Adam stumbled toward it like a drunk man chasing his shadow, lungs burning and vision blurring at the edges. The entrance was choked with mist and vines, overgrown and breathing like it was alive.

He pushed through, gasping for air. And there he was. Dilly stood perfectly still just beyond the chain-link fence; eyes locked on Adam with unnatural calm.

The fence was intact.

No breaks.

No gaps.

No branches hanging overhead.

There was no way in . . . but Dilly was inside.

As if he had phased through the wire.

As if the rules of the world no longer applied to him. As if he was something more than animal now.

Something that didn't belong.

"What the cuck?" Adam gasped, collapsing onto the gravel next to the fence. Sweat soaked through his shirt, and his chest heaved like it was trying to punch through his ribs.

"How the hell did your stupid monkey-ass get in there?" he slurred loudly, but even his own voice sounded small beneath the watching silence.

There they were. Just the two of them, facing off once again in the heavy silence of the night. No cries, no screeches, no noise at all. Only their eyes met, and somehow that was enough. There was a knowing in the gaze, an awareness far too deep for the moment.

Then Dilly moved.

A slow, deliberate gesture toward Adam's chest pocket. Adam followed the motion, then noticed the banana Emma had slipped him earlier. He let out a low, dry laugh that sounded slightly unhinged, and dragged his wrist across his sweaty brow.

"Here, take it," Adam muttered with sour breath, shoving the fruit through the chain-link fence. "You must be starving after all that mystical escape artist shit."

Dilly accepted it with careful fingers, almost tenderly. He peeled it back and bit in, chewing slowly, methodically, like he was trying to remember what food was; like a newborn discovering taste. Adam, caught between fear and fascination, reached for his phone. He tried to snap a few photos of the chimp, but the images were all dark smudges and shadows. He tapped the flash on. The next click lit up Dilly's face. The chimpanzee froze. His eyes locked onto the device with a new intensity. No longer seeing Adam at all. Just the phone. His stare deepened, burning through the flash as if it were a flame. Then, with the same eerie calm he used to point at the banana, Dilly lifted a hand and pointed again. But this time, he wasn't asking for food.

"You like this?" Adam said from the other side of the fence. "I must be drunker than I thought. You wanna see what this thing can do?" Adam asked as he played music from it. The song in the queue was Coldplay's *Up in Flames*. The melody drifted between them like smoke. Dilly didn't blink. He didn't breathe. He listened. Adam started swiping through his apps, laughing to his drunken self as he opened YouTube, then Candy Crush, flipping to Instagram, TikTok, Snapchat. He tried out a few filters, distorted his face, made it into a dog, a clown, a demon. Each app drew some new flicker of reaction from Dilly. Curiosity, recognition, even fascination. But none of it was enough. Dilly's fingers reached through the fence. Palm up, fingers twitching. Not demanding but pleading. The moan that left his throat was almost human. A cry of desperation.

Adam hesitated. Every nerve in his body said to stop. But the buzz from the bourbon blurred the warnings. He didn't want to admit he was scared. Didn't want to admit the monkey had some kind of spell over him.

"Alright," he said quietly. "Make sure you give it back."

With a nervous glance, Adam slid the phone through the diamond-shaped hole in the fence. The device disappeared into those dark, leathery hands like a relic being received by a priest.

But then something changed.

The air shifted.

The desert warmth gave way to a strange chill, like a door had opened somewhere that shouldn't exist in this world. Adam felt the hair rise on his arms. Dilly stood up onto two feet. The animal stepped back from the fence, still holding the phone. Then he looked up, and grinned. But it was something cosmic, almost supernatural. An expression not in God's creation. His gaze narrowed, his mouth twitched into a half-smirk that didn't belong to primal instinct. It was as if the curiosity had learned how to lie, as if behind those yellow, liquid eyes a calculating thought had clicked into place. It was a knowing grin, sly and malevolent, as if he had just been handed the key to something unholy.

"Okay, monkey. Give it back," Adam said, this time with an edge in his voice.

But Dilly turned without a sound and vanished into the undergrowth, the glow of the screen bouncing light against his fur as he slipped away like a dream turned into a nightmare. Adam watched in disbelief as the enclosure's clearing fell into a bruised silence, as if the earth itself had stopped its pulse. In that moment, the night reset. Old rules of the life he knew burning away with the light of his phone. Whatever stepped into those shadows would not be the same creature; something deeper had taken the reins of the banana boy's life now.

"Holy shit," Adam muttered to himself, suddenly very sober.

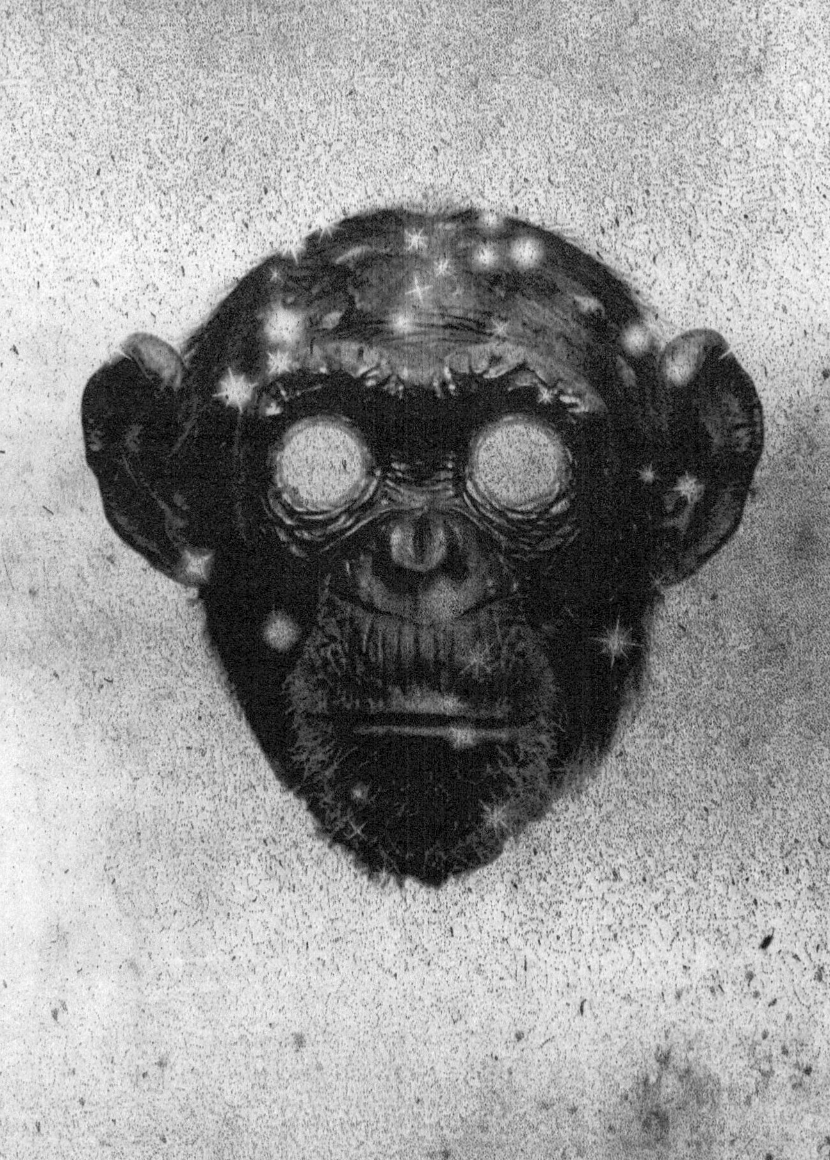

"Oh no, I see
A spider web is tangled up with me"

Coldplay

Chapter 14

Chapter 15

Emma opened her door and hit the light switch, expecting the warm hum of her apartment to greet her.

Nothing. She flicked the switch again.

Still nothing.

The dark swallowed everything.

With a sigh and a rising tension crawling up her spine, she pulled out her phone and turned on the flashlight. The beam cut through the musty air and landed on something that made her breath catch in her throat. Webbing. A gnarled, unnatural tapestry weaved as if from some other time and space. It draped across every corner of her home like a silken disease, stretched from the fridge to the bookshelves, across the windows, clinging to the ceiling fan and tangling around the chairs.

The texture wasn't quite like any web she'd seen. It looked more like decaying fabric strung together by something with patience and intention. Her hand came to her mouth, as if to keep her jaw from falling off her face entirely.

"What in the fuckberry . . ." she muttered, stepping forward with caution as the webs brushed against her jeans, already wound up to her knees.

There's no way Munchkin could do this?

The air was sweet and rotting at the same time. A sharp note of banana clung to it, so thick she could almost taste it. She placed her bag on the kitchen island, web-covered and pulsing like it might be breathing. The moment the bag touched the surface, the webbing reacted. As if she alerted its maker of her presence.

There was a shift.

Then another one, ever so slightly.

Then she heard it.

A noise that sounded like something dragging across linoleum. Wet and slow, but not footsteps. A squelch. Followed by a low chittering moan, a sound that didn't belong in her world. Or this world.

Emma edged her flashlight toward the sound and froze. It was crawling.

No, walking.

A banana peel, yellowed and glistening, but emptied of its fruit.

Its flaps moved like legs, sharp and segmented, carrying the hollow skin like a spider across the sticky floor. It weaved a fresh trail of silk behind it, methodically and unbothered by her presence. It didn't flinch.

All of Emma's experience in animal handling was the only thing that kept her from completely losing it. She didn't run. Something about the sheer wrongness of it all locked her in place. But the fear was too real to allow panic. She moved slowly, reaching for a mason jar from the shelf with a shaking hand. Inch by inch, she crept forward. And in one smooth motion, she brought the jar down over the creature. It snapped its body upward, slapping at the glass as if it knew it had been trapped. The banana-spider scurried inside its new prison, testing the edges, brushing its limbs against the surface, twisting and twitching as it searched for escape. Emma tapped the glass once. Then again.

"What the fuck are you?" she whispered.

The jar twitched in her hands, as if trying to answer.

"In the night, I lie and look up at you"

Coldplay

Chapter 15

Chapter 16

Adam lay in bed wide-eyed and motionless beneath the heavy quilt while the early morning began its routine without him. From his sister's room came the soft hum of music as she readied for school. Somewhere above, the attic shifted with restless creaks, and down the block, a door slammed like a gunshot through the stillness. The dawn was alive, louder than he could bear, and every sound was a fresh reminder of what he'd lost.

That fucking monkey.

But really, Adam was furious with himself. Another drunken mistake changing the script of his life. Furious that he'd been stupid enough, drunk enough, desperate enough to hand over his phone like it was nothing. *I can't tell Jeff. I can't tell Emma.*

I sure as hell can't tell Ruby. His thoughts spiraled in a downward tumble, slamming into one another like freight cars. *I need a phone. Maybe I take it from Ruby's savings. Ask her? Just grab it? She won't know. God, what kind of person even thinks like that?*

The guilt grew like mold in his chest. His thoughts were sour and sweaty, scraping against the inside of his skull like claws. Frustration plucked his brain like a banjo strung too tight. He was spiraling, helpless, hopeless, again. Then something inside him clicked.

Maybe it was Jeff's ridiculous speech from earlier. Maybe it was the sheer absurdity of losing his phone to a chimpanzee.

Or maybe it was just survival instinct.

Either way, Adam sat up, bones heavy, and mind ablaze with a plan.

Tomorrow night, I'll go back. I'll bring bananas. I'll wait him out. He'll drop it. I'll grab it. Done.

It sounded just crazy enough to work, because without his phone, without music, without the picture, the weight of grief processing in his head was unbearable. He needed something, anything. His eyes drifted across the room to the mason jar of sharpened pencils, standing at attention. Next to them sat his old sketchbooks, worn at the edges, bent from years of being shoved under mattresses and forgotten in closets. He didn't want to draw. Didn't want to sink into that vulnerable space, but his hands were already reaching. As if they knew before he did what he needed.

The book opened with a whisper of paper and charcoal dust. The blank page stared back like the void itself, the first dragon every artist must face. Adam hesitated for a breath, then another. And then, his pencil did the rest. It scratched across the page slowly, carefully, without conscious thought. His brain had no say in it. It was instinct and muscle memory as the lines curved, and shadows formed.

And when he was done ... there he was, the chimpanzee.

"Confusion that never stops"

Coldplay

Chapter 17

Adam awoke in the late afternoon, the sun already halfway through its descent behind the Arizona hills. His body ached in the quiet way regret does. He had fallen asleep with a pencil clenched in one hand and his sketchbook in the other, as if the drawings had dragged him under. It surprised him how sleep had found him without Coldplay, without the photo, without the weight of that damn phone pulsing against his thigh.

But as the drunken fog began to burn off his vision, Adam blinked and froze. His room wasn't his room anymore.

The walls were no longer bare. Every inch of space had been plastered page after page, torn straight from his sketchbook, but altered. Twisted.

As if someone had gutted his private thoughts and reassembled them with surgical malice. And on every sheet . . . Dilly's fucking eyes. Staring. Dozens of them. Maybe hundreds? Each one, watching him.

His breath caught.

Jesus Christ.

He stepped closer as the paper crinkled in the light breeze from the ceiling fan, like dry skin shifting. He reached out, tore one down, then another. The lines were all familiar to him, but wrong. Something seemed more visually obsessive. The kind of art you don't remember making, but somehow still feel responsible for. It was as if something had borrowed him, wore his skin, and left only charcoaled evidence behind. Eyes that watched.

He dressed slowly, with great discomfort in his room. But there was a feeling of purpose that settled over him. Today, he would fix it. He will sneak into the zoo, find Dilly, and take back what is his. The purpose made his limbs feel lighter. He sat at the edge of his bed, sliding on his socks, one at a time, rehearsing the plan. Bananas. Patience. Recovery. Rock and roll.

He stood to grab his sneakers from the closet and froze. The clothes in his closet were swaying. Barely, but noticeably. As if someone were pressing gently against them from behind, breathing shallow, trying not to be found. Adam's heartbeat sounded in his ears, then his throat, then his fingertips. He took one step closer, watching as the flannels shifted like soft waves on hangers. He wasn't sure if it was real; he wasn't sure if he was in the moment. "Hello?" he called, voice cracking through the silence. There was a pause.

A whisper answered him. "Hello?" Soft and fragile. Like it was trying the word on for the first time. Adam jolted upright, instinct gripping him like a vice. He turned fast, reaching for the baseball bat that leaned against his bedpost.

It reached out. A black, leathery hand, long-fingered and primal, creeping through the curtain of coats.

It was Dilly. First came the black, skeletal fingers, curling over the edge like hooks. Then the grizzled arm, matted with filth and muscle. And finally, the animal's wretched face. Adam heard a low grunt, thick with syllables and spit, something between a growl and a word.

The demon leaned in close, lips barely moving, and whispered, *"Switch."*

Adam opened his mouth to scream, but a new voice stopped him.

"Adam! What the balls?" It was Ruby's voice, panicked and close by. "Adam!"

Everything cracked. The closet vanished. The coats collapsed inward. Adam blinked awake, and he was on the kitchen floor, face pressed to the tile, body smeared in something soft. The smell hit him first . . . banana. Overripe, fermented. Peels all around him like wet yellow confetti, celebrating his downward spiral to madness. His hands were tacky. His chest bare. His body . . . naked. He scrambled to cover himself as Ruby stared at him in horror.

"What the hell is happening to you?!" she cried. No sass, no sarcasm. Just fear as she looked at her brother like he was a stranger.

Adam stumbled to his feet wide-eyed and sprinted down the hallway, slamming his bedroom door behind him. Sending a wave through the hundreds of Dilly eyes that hung like flags in his room. He could no longer decode what was a dream as he stared at the illustrations, and what was reality. He collapsed against the door, gasping. The shame was thicker than the heat in the room, his sister seeing him covered in pulp. He looked down at his hands, coated in mush, they shook as if they'd betrayed him. Then came a knock.

"Adam," Ruby said, voice quiet through the cheap wood, "what's going on with you?"

Adam swallowed hard and lied. Another lie. "I'm just tired, okay? It's sleepwalking. I'm fine."

"You're not," she said, cracking, "and if you don't pull yourself together, I don't think I can—"

"Can what?" he said, with bated breath.

"I don't think I can . . . stay here?" she whispered. "Uncle Jeff said . . . he said maybe I should move in with him."

Adam closed his eyes. *Of course Jeff said that.* "Jeff is wrong."

"Maybe we both should," she said, voice hopeful, but Adam couldn't give her what she wanted.

"Just give me more time," he pleaded. "Please, let me prove to you I can do this. Let me take care of you."

Silence, then footsteps. Followed by the front door, which clicked open and shut.

Adam stood alone. His eyes drifted toward the closet. If the artwork was real, then was the primate intruder? Slowly, he crossed the room and yanked it open. Only clothes. But there, between the boots and jackets, was space. A man-sized gap where something should be. The hangers were parted. The shoes nudged aside. As if something had been standing there . . . waiting.

But there in the chasm between the shoes, was what could only be described as a sprinkling. A dusting or light snowfall from a small closet storm piled in the openness. The banana boy traced his eyes upward, as if looking for the cloud which could have shit this out, only to be confronted with a small peephole in the center of his closet. Adam stood confused and angered until his breath began to shake, his stomach twisting on itself. He slammed the door with everything he had. The mirror cracked on impact, multiplying the eyes of the jungle devil as they watched the banana boy.

"Fucking monkey!" he screamed, chest heaving.

"Yes I feel a little bit nervous
Yes I feel nervous and I cannot relax
How come they're out to get us
How come they're out when they don't know the facts"

Coldplay

Chapter 17

Chapter 18

Ruby sat on the banana-yellow school bus; her phone clutched tightly in her hands. The bus bounced and rattled as it made its way down the road, but Ruby was too absorbed in her screen to notice. Trying to distract her failing heart from the sky falling in her life.

Between TikTok reels of Coldplay's *Adventure Of A Lifetime* music video, where the band embodied chimpanzees, to photos of her dead parents. She was looking at anything to distract her emotions. Then the spirit of *fuck it* came over her as her fingers moved in a mechanical rhythm, scrolling, tapping, her eyes darting across each search result as she Googled something—anything—to find out what could be happening to her brother.

Her thoughts swirled around his strange behavior, their uncertain future, and the deep pit of fear that seemed to gnaw at her insides.

She typed, each search more desperate than the last, hoping for something, anything, that might make sense of it all.

"Bananas rubbed on body"

"What do bananas represent in mental illness"

"Bananas and men"

"Bananas and trauma"

"Parent's death bananas"

"What do bananas represent in our subconscious?"

"Are bananas bad?"

The phrases seemed ridiculous as they appeared on her screen, absurd even. She could feel her cheeks flush with embarrassment as she quickly scrolled past crude images of men shoving bananas down their pants, their smug grins mocking her search.

Ruby turned her head, pretending to look out the window, to make sure no one was looking over her shoulder. She didn't want anyone to see her, or worse, to see her searching for answers to something so . . . strange.

But then, as the bus's wheels hummed against the pavement, she stumbled upon something that made her heart race. It was a link to a psychological article, buried deep among the clutter of useless junk, but something about it caught her attention. She clicked the bait.

Subject: Urgent Request: Transfer of Last Chimpanzee from Closing Sanctuary

Dear Nancy,

First and foremost, I want to express my deepest condolences for the loss of Mr. Teegan. I was truly saddened to hear the news. Bryan was a remarkable individual, and his dedication to animal welfare was evident in every conversation we had. I can only imagine how difficult this time must be for you and everyone at Chimp Haven. Please know that my thoughts are with you all.

Regarding the matter at hand, I appreciate your kind offer to reconsider the terms and the financial support you've proposed for the transfer and compensation. We are very grateful for your generosity during this incredibly challenging period. As of now, the board and I agree that the well-being of the chimpanzee will now be a top priority, and I am confident we can work together to ensure it receives the best possible care moving forward.

Let me know when you'd like to ship the chimpanzee,
and all other pertinent dates and details. I'd like to
arrange a financial call as well to finalize all loose ends.

Thank you again for your understanding and for
honoring Bryan's memory in this way.

Warm sympathies,
Jeffrey Harrison, Director | Prescott AZ Zoo

"And I will try to fix you"

Coldplay

Chapter 18

Chapter 19

Ruby's eyes scanned the text, her breath slowing as the words on the screen seemed to blur together. She read them again, then again. The weight of what she was reading settled in her stomach like a stone.

> *Bananas, while commonly praised for their nutritional benefits, can pose specific considerations for mental health, particularly concerning cerebral and subconscious functions. High in potassium, bananas can disrupt electrolyte balance when consumed excessively, potentially impairing neurotransmitter regulation critical for cognitive processes and subconscious functions. This imbalance may manifest as cognitive fog, disorientation, or disturbances in subconscious thought patterns.*

Her mouth went dry as she tried to process the information. A hot shiver crept down her spine. The words felt like they were digging a hole beneath her feet—too real, too terrifying, too close. Her brother's obsession with bananas ... was it somehow connected to his mental state? The thought made her stomach twist like a bag of snakes.

For a moment, her finger hovered over the screen. She could hear the heavy mechanics of the bus, the sound of muffled voices from the other kids, but it felt distant, like the world around her was fading. She wanted to stop. Part of her screamed to put the phone away, to ignore it all. Losing their parents had already made her hollow. The idea of losing Adam too, the only family she had left, was an ache she couldn't bear. But as the chaos of her thoughts swirled, something inside her urged her to read on. There's got to be an answer here, she thought, something that makes sense.

She scrolled down; each swipe felt like a deeper level of hell.

Bananas throughout history have been known to be symbols of poor luck and misfortune. Bananas are not allowed to be brought aboard any ship or vessel, as when ships have sunk to the depths, all that floats on the surface above was the banana. Like beacons of death and tragedy they . . .

The words seemed to darken before her eyes, their implications twisting in her chest. It felt like the air around her had thickened, pressing in on her from all sides. Ruby's heart was in her throat. *Was this why Adam was acting the way he was?*

Frantically, she shoved the phone down onto the empty seat next to her, her hands trembling. She pressed her palms to her eyes, but the words clung to her mind. She could almost feel them, the weight of them, heavy and oppressive. What happened to the Adam who wiped his boogers on her and watched horror movies until they passed out? But now, Adam's bizarre behavior, the bananas, the way he seemed to be spiraling. What kind of sick game is his subconscious playing with him? Her mind raced, unable to quiet the questions, the fear.

She felt the need to fix it, to make it stop, to make sense of it. But nothing made sense, and that was the scariest part. She felt utterly helpless, and the idea of not knowing what was happening to her brother, the idea of being powerless to help him, felt like a boulder was tied to her insides.

With a sudden, desperate impulse, she grabbed the phone again, her fingers shaky as she tapped out a message.

Ruby stared at the screen, her words staring back at her. She meant every word, but at that moment, she wasn't sure if her brother would even understand or agree. Would he see it as a cry for help? Or would it only push him further away?

She hit send. If she knew one thing about Adam, he was a slow text responder, if he responded at all. But then an ellipsis appeared.

Then it disappeared. A maddening flicker on her screen. *Is he reading it? Is he responding?* Her fingers tapped nervously against the phone's edge as the seconds stretched on. Each passing moment felt like an eternity.

Then, finally, a text came through from Adam's phone.

"And though you might be gone,
and the world may not know
Still I see you, celestial"

Coldplay

Chapter 19

Chapter 20

Adam slipped back into the zoo easily, since he hadn't turned in his spare keys yet. And the zoo still had no night shift guard to replace him, even if it was temporary. The zoo was unnervingly still, as if the animals had all fallen into a collective slumber, their usual sounds replaced by the soft rustling of leaves in the hot Arizona wind. The air felt drier than in the past nights, broken only by the occasional creak of metal gates or the distant call of a nocturnal creature.

Shadows stretched across the paths, swallowing the familiar structures, leaving behind a sense of something hidden just beyond the darkness. Adam did the best he could to dodge every security camera, unsure if Jeff had replaced the broken laptop.

In his backpack were as many bundles of bananas as he could fit from the grocery store. He unpacked each one and laid them out before the chimpanzee enclosure as if they were an offering to the ape gods. Adam recited the plan, *Bananas. Patience. Recovery. Rock and roll.*

Once neatly placed before the chain-link wall, Adam waited. "Come on, come on, you little bitch," he whispered to himself in the darkness, the misters cooling his hot temper. After a few minutes, Adam began to cry out Dilly's name as playfully as his anger would allow him.

When he didn't appear, Adam began to look deeper into the large enclosure, desperately trying to see through the night for the demon monkey.

But there in the distance, he saw him, it was Dilly.

Dilly's face was aglow with baby blue hue as Adam watched the monkey scrolling away on his phone. He couldn't believe it. *How is any of this possible? How is the battery not dead? How is this monkey an Apple Bar Genius? How does this fucking monkey still have my phone and hasn't replaced it with a handful of his own shit? Do I go in there? Do I shoot the fucker?*

"Dilly!" Adam screamed, getting the animal's attention. The chimp's eyes, which were fixated on the phone, were now on him. Now that Adam had Dilly's attention, he didn't know what to do with it. Logic told him this animal couldn't understand jack shit. But his gut told him that this animal was playing a dangerous game.

Adam grabbed hold of the chain-link, and all he could do was shake it hard in annoyance as he watched Dilly turn completely away from him and continue his activity on Adam's phone. The blue glowing silhouette of the chimpanzee teased him from beyond the fence.

Emma had googled every goddamn site on the internet for some sort of explanation to the spider peel. Hours of scrolling. Pages of inconclusive garbage. Each click felt like a slow, grinding erosion of her sanity, like the frantic tapping of her fingers was wearing away at her mind, each search result more nonsensical than the last. Nothing made sense. Nothing fit.

Site after site, cigarette after cigarette, Emma's brain was slowly turning to mush. She'd even tried searching the dark web, desperate for something, anything, that could explain the impossibility of what she was holding in her hand. The spider peel. A creature she trapped inside the glass jar. Was it a demon? A fairy from Banana Land? A key? A god? But in her search, most of what she found were vague references to occult conspiracies and cryptic folklore, which only made her question whether she'd accidentally stumbled into some kind of living nightmare.

She stared at the jar, eyes narrowing. "How the fuck are you a thing?" she hissed at it. The spider peel's thick and browning skin moved gracefully. Its body flipped and shifted inside, bouncing slightly with every tap of her finger against the glass. She felt her mind spiral. *Was this it? Was this the end of reason? Was there a giant zoo boat and a great flood? Was the purpose of life just a joke, a cosmic riddle with no punchline? Could God even be? Am I even real? Was this room real?*

The questions came fast now, a flood of absurdities crashing into each other, making her dizzy. The creature writhed with its yellow alien limbs curling in jerking motions that made her stomach churn. With each tap, its skin pulled taut, like rubber being stretched, skin shimmering in the faint light of the kitchen. The other creature, Munchkin, her stolen tarantula—the poor bastard—seemed to be losing his mind, too, as he bounced around in his aquarium, bashing against the sides, hoping to escape . . . whatever this was.

Emma jumped to her feet, slamming her laptop shut with a force that made the table rattle. She couldn't sit there any longer, staring at that screen at those incomprehensible answers. She needed to do something. Anything. She grabbed the broom from the corner and began sweeping up the sticky webbing of the spider peel, frantic, as if cleaning the apartment could somehow rid her of this curse. But the more she scrubbed, the more she wiped, the less the place felt like hers. As if the act of cleaning wasn't just an attempt to rid the place of dust, but of the literal insanity. She wiped at the corners, at the dust bunnies, at the webs, but as she scrubbed, she uncovered things she wasn't prepared for.

The framed photos on the walls began to reveal themselves, but not the ones she remembered. Not the ones that were originally hung there. The smiling faces from past hiking adventures, from backpacking trips across Europe . . . gone.

In their place stood Emma, in a white gown. A soft glow around her. Her face was radiant, unfamiliar in a way, but her eyes were wide with joy. But the second photo, her hand on her large pink belly, her pregnant belly, smiling down at it. The roundness, the happiness, the pregnancy that changed everything.

What the hell is happening?

Her breath caught in her throat. She wiped harder, frantic, as the images began to shift before her eyes, impossible moments playing out in those frames, memories that felt so distant, yet so immediate. She felt the tears prick at her eyes, blurring the scene before her. She reached for another frame, another moment, but the cloth she used to wipe away the spider webs had become sticky, the fibers clinging to the glass, to her hands, like something alive, as though it was a part of whatever sick joke was unfolding.

"No. How could this be?!" Emma shouted to the frames. Her thoughts began to swim, and the world seemed to tilt around her. Nothing made sense. She wiped again, and the frame shifted. A picture of her, with him and their unborn child. The man she threw a wedding ring back at years ago. His hand on her shoulder. Her hand cradling his.

"Stop . . ." Emma whispered, the word more of a sob than anything. "Please, stop."

The floor felt like it was webbing under her feet, the walls closing in as if they were spiders wanting to feed on her. And then, a soft, primal moan. Emma turned, eyes wide, and her heart dropped to her stomach. The spider peel trapped in its glass prison. Making a new noise, a sound that sent shivers through her skin. It was almost like a whisper, a low, vibrating hum that seemed to reverberate through her bones. The creature had no eyes, but Emma knew it was staring at her. Locked on her, and for the first time, Emma felt it was the one orchestrating all of this.

It wasn't just a creature anymore. It was something much more dangerous.

As if it was there, as if it watched everything that created guilt in her life.

Subject: Urgent Request: Transfer of Last
Chimpanzee from Closing Sanctuary

Nancy,

I hope this email finds you well, though I have to
express my disappointment regarding the way the
chimpanzee's transfer was handled. As you know, we
had agreed on finalizing the details ahead of time—
specifically around the shipping dates, transportation,
and compensation—as well as a proper communication
plan to ensure everything went smoothly. However, the
chimp showed up here without any prior notice, details,
or warning. We were completely unprepared for its
arrival, and it has caused significant disruptions to our
operations and the care arrangements we had in place.
I have called numerous times, with no avail.

I'm sure you understand that receiving an animal of this
size and complexity without any logistical communication creates a serious challenge. We had anticipated a
collaborative process, with all parties fully informed at

every step, to ensure both the chimp's well-being and smooth transition. This lack of foresight and communication has created unnecessary complications that we are now scrambling to resolve.

I would like to request that we address this issue urgently. I would appreciate it if you could provide immediate clarification on the financial details, including any changes to the agreed-upon compensation and logistical support.

Please let me know when would be a good time for us to have a call and resolve this. I'm eager to get this situation back on track, but I do need more clarity and communication moving forward.

Thank you for your urgent attention to this matter.

Jeffrey Harrison, Director | Prescott AZ Zoo

"And the spies came out of the water
But you're feeling so bad 'cause you know
That the spies hide out in every corner."

Coldplay

Chapter 20

Chapter 21

Ruby came home from school expecting her brother Adam to be readying himself for his night shift at the zoo. She entered quietly, almost instinctively, unsure if he was still sleeping or sprawled out naked on the floor in banana paste. Their relationship had always been unpredictable, especially lately, and she couldn't help but feel a flicker of hesitation for what she could be walking into.

"Dipshit?" she called out softly, her voice hesitant as she dropped her backpack with a thud on the floor. The silence was heavy and oppressive, seeping into the walls of their house. It was a subtle, constant reminder of how much their family had shrunk in recent years, a feeling that had become more pronounced with each passing day.

But as the silence stretched on, Ruby felt a rush of relief. She wasn't sure how she could help Adam, though she wanted to. Needed to. She didn't know how to reach him anymore, not with the way he had been acting. Since their parents' death, she was the first to admit that he was on his own grief journey, one that Ruby felt helpless to follow. One that Ruby felt a growing bitterness toward.

She shrugged off her unease and made her way into the kitchen, the familiar rhythm of routine settling over her. Maybe she could grab a snack and kill some time scrolling through TikTok garbage until Adam came back from wherever he had gone. She rummaged through the fridge and found bologna and cheese sticks, her dad's favorite snack, and one of Ruby's last lingering connections to him. He used to call them his "cheese shivs" and pretended to stab her as they ate. A strange ritual that turned eating into something almost sacred.

The kitchen was eerily quiet, save for the steady song of the refrigerator and the occasional drip of water from the faucet into the sink, which was half-filled with the stale remnants of yesterday's dishes. The overhead light flickered once, then settled into a steady glow that felt too harsh, almost sterile in the silence. For a second, the kitchen seemed to shudder, like the house was holding its breath.

On the counter, a dull knife lay beside a scattered pile of coffee grounds and wilted vegetables. It wasn't the food or the mess that made Ruby's skin crawl. It was the unsettling sensation that something was off, as though she were waiting for something to happen. Ruby stopped mid-motion, her fingers hovering over the shivs as she listened to her surroundings.

"Adam?" she called again, louder this time, but the sound of her own voice felt strange, unnatural, like she was trying to fill a void, or scare off unseen demons.

Suddenly, the sharp ding of a notification from her phone broke the silence.

It was a message from Adam.

switch

Ruby texted back, beyond confused.

Huh?? wut are you tryin to say???

fuggin cockwaffle bruh

I have a dirty little secret. It's about mommy and daddy.

Ruby's stomach dropped as she stared at the message. She took a slow, cautious bite of her snack, as if it might somehow help her process the cryptic words. Her teeth sank into the bologna and cheese, but her thoughts couldn't help but race. The whole thing felt . . . off. She chewed slowly, staring down at the screen in confusion.

"Da fuck?" she whispered under her breath.

She typed back with a shaky hand.

Okayyy, freak

Another bite, then the smell hit her. It was an unmistakable, gut-churning stench. Like the barnyard smell of shit and nauseating animals, heavy and cloying. Ruby froze mid-chew, her stomach turning from the stench.

She dropped the food onto the counter, pushing it away as if it could somehow contaminate her. The smell filled her lungs, thick and suffocating. It clung to the walls and seemed to press in from every corner, making her skin crawl.

And then . . . *splat.*

The sound of something wet and heavy hitting the floor echoed from the living room. Ruby's heart skipped a beat. Another splat followed, this time hitting the wall behind her with a sickening thud. She turned, her pulse spiking.

Whizz.

A dark splatter shot past her head, the force of it so close she could feel her hair wave in its path. Splat. It hit the wallpaper with a sickening splatter, the yellow floral design now stained with dark, oozing shit.

Ruby's eyes widened in shock as she attempted to back away, every instinct screaming at her to flee. But she was frozen in place, rooted to the spot. The room seemed to grow colder, the smell intensifying, as if the very air around her was thick with rot. Another *whizz* and a *splat*, this time, on her chest, then her thigh.

"Stop it!" Ruby screamed, her voice rising in panic, as she scrambled to pull out her phone to call Adam. Then she heard it, the ringer . . . Adam's ringer, coming from the living room.

Ruby's heart pounded in her chest as she turned toward the dark living room, where the sound of her brother's ringtone vibrated through the walls. In the half-darkness of the room, she saw the soft, eerie glow of her incoming call. Her phone buzzed in her hand as the call rang on.

"Adam, you dog fart! What the fuck is going on with all this shit?!" Ruby shouted, her voice shaking with frustration and confusion.

Then, the grunts came.

It wasn't Adam. It was something else, something raw and guttural. A dark, throaty hoot that cut the air. Ruby's blood ran cold as she heard it again, closer this time.

Before she could react, another *whizz*, *splat*, *plop* and this one broke across her face with the sickening force of a head shot.

Ruby gasped, her mouth open in shock as the thick, putrid black shit splattered across her face, the warmth of it seeping into her skin. She screamed in disgust, wiping frantically at her face with the sleeve of her sweater. Another throw landed on her cheek and into her mouth.

At that moment, something shifted. A shadow, a blur of motion from the living room. Whatever was there rushed forward in the darkness, knocking over a table and a lamp crashing to the ground. The sound of the back door crashed open. Ruby could hear it, something large and heavy darting through the yard, fading into the evening.

Her phone buzzed again, and Ruby lifted it, still trembling, unable to pull her eyes from the chaos that had just unfolded. She glanced at the screen which was also smeared in feces.

It was another text from Adam.

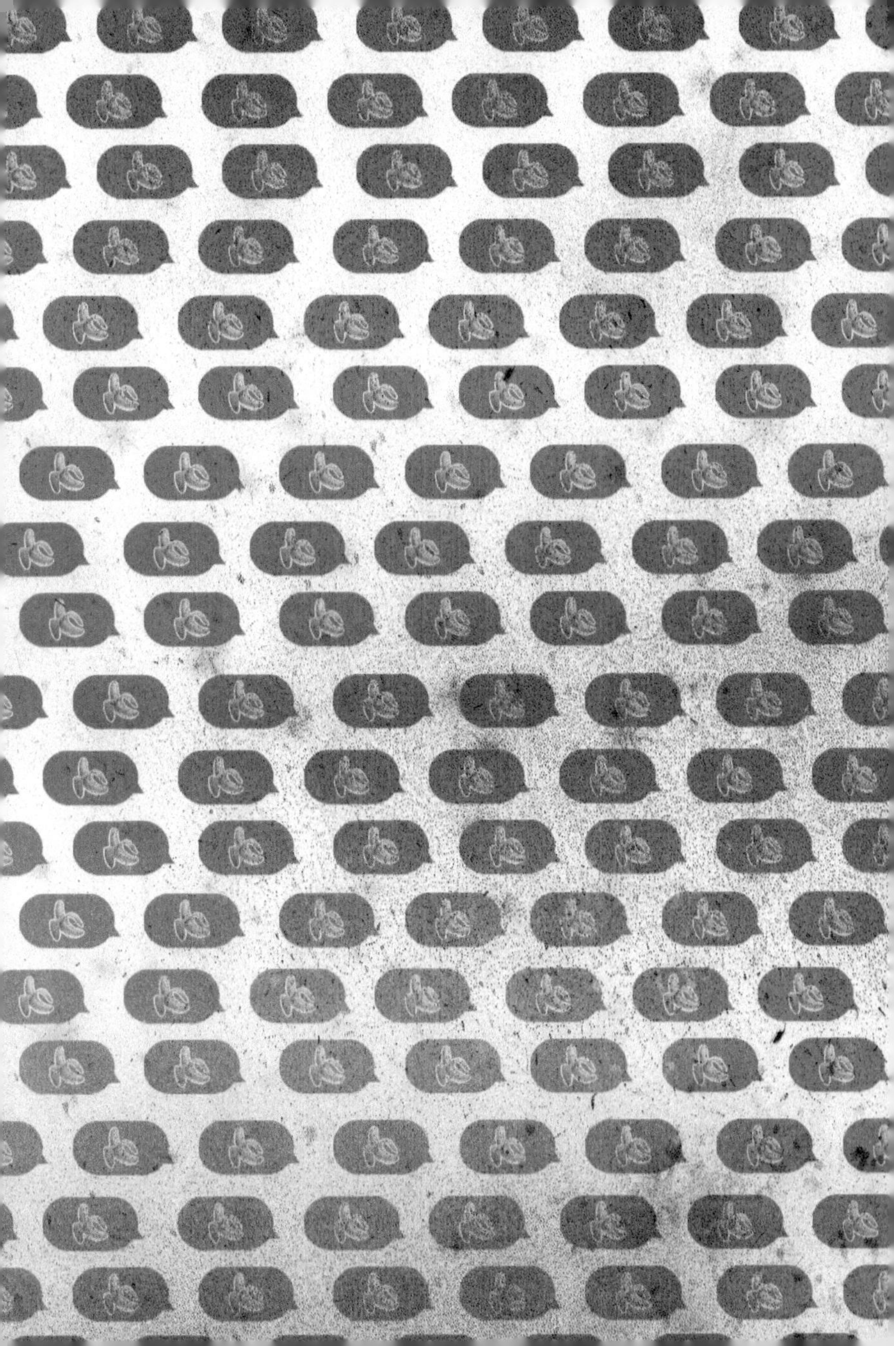

"Stood on a sea of pain,
Let it rain, let it rain, let it rain.
I'll be back on my feet again"

Coldplay

"I need your keys, Adam. We're going to have to let you go," Jeff said, leaning forward in his chair, his eyes steady but tired, like a man delivering a verdict he'd feared for a long time. His voice was calm, matter-of-fact. But Adam could hear the unspoken weight behind it. The creaks coming from his wooden chair filled the silence between them.

Adam reached into his pocket and removed the last remaining relics of his employment at The Prescott Zoo. He didn't say a word, just nodded, his neck stiff with the gravity of it all. The words were nothing new, truthfully, he'd been expecting this since he started. The disappointment in his uncle's eyes wasn't a surprise. Adam had let everyone down; that much was obvious. He always expected the worst now, like a sword hanging perpetually over his head.

"The staff can't know I'm playing favorites," Jeff continued, his voice low as he sifted through the thin pretense of professionalism. "If I keep you on after an error this large . . . it'll make everyone else feel like they can get away with anything. I can't have that. Zoos must be run tightly and efficiently. I know you understand this."

Adam's chest tightened. The words hit like blunt objects, dull and more painful than expected.

"Can I ask you something, Adam?" Jeff asked, one eyebrow lifting higher than the other. Adam nodded, crossing his arms in his familiar defensive pose.

"Why do you think I'm in your life?"

Adam couldn't understand the question, and Jeff knew it by reading his face.

"I mean, none of this is random. Your parents, your job now, your demons. None of this is a cosmic, arbitrary accident."

"Okay?" Adam said, wanting the moment to suffocate and die.

"I'm here to watch you and your sister. My job is to keep an eye out for you, and I take that very, very seriously. But if you hide yourself from me, it's harder to see what's really going on. As your boss, I must discipline you, as your uncle, I get to watch over you."

Adam could feel a low-level rage burning within him, a fury in the form of a hum buzzed from somewhere inside of himself. He didn't care about the job anymore. Hell, he didn't even care about the firing. But the fact that this came from Jeff, his limp dicked uncle, made everything suck harder. Then his mind swung to thoughts of losing Ruby, and everything that was kindled within him cooled.

"I get it," Adam said, his voice small, distant. He kept his gaze fixed on the floor, his eyes blurry from lack of sleep, from the spiraling banana thoughts that hadn't stopped running through his head in days. What was worse, losing his job, being fired by family, or the nagging suspicion that even this was somehow connected to that fucking monkey? Jeff didn't notice the flicker of panic that passed through Adam's eyes. He was already thinking ahead, considering the logistics of it all.

"And we agree that I should take Ruby for the rest of the summer," Jeff said, completely shifting the conversation, pulling Adam's attention in a way he wasn't ready for. "This way you can focus on getting something locked in. No distractions. Become a man. I think it's for the best."

Adam's blood turned cold. He stood up, the chair scraping loudly against the floor. "Wait, what?" His voice was a little too sharp, too loud for the calm office.

Jeff looked up at him, unfazed. "Adam, what am I missing? You said it yourself," he said, as though this was the most natural thing in the world. "You said, Ruby's better off here with me. You need to get yourself together, to take her for the summer."

Adam's mind scrambled. "I never said that." The words tumbled out before he could stop them. "What the hell are you talking about?"

Jeff didn't flinch. Just a raised brow of confusion. A tick of the toothpick. He pulled his phone out of his pocket, tapping the screen a few times, scrolling through something Adam couldn't see. Adam's stomach dropped, his pulse quickening as a sinking feeling washed over him. Something was very wrong. He could feel it in his gut. His uncle held up the phone, revealing a text from Adam's old number. Clear as day, crystal, no mystery, no fuzziness.

A message that detailed, in simple but unmistakable terms, the suggestion that Ruby should stay with Jeff for the summer. "Ruby needs to be with you. I need to focus on myself," the text read. Sent twenty-four hours ago. Adam's skin prickled, his breath catching in his throat like fire. He felt like he was suffocating, as if the world was breaking around him. This wasn't possible. He didn't send this. His hands shook as he tried to process what he was seeing, but the words wouldn't stop swimming in his vision. How could a monkey do this?!

"Adam," Jeff said, a little more urgently now, his eyes narrowing. "Tell me what's going on. I'm here for you. I'm not going to let you keep spiraling like this."

Adam opened his mouth, trying to force words out, but nothing came. His tongue was dry as a leaf, his heart beating too fast. He could feel the panic rising again, a wave of heat that made his skin feel tight and foreign. "I . . . I don't know," he muttered, his voice cracking. "I don't know what's happening."

"Are you drinking again?" Jeff asked, trying to find the diagnosis.

There was a beat of silence.

Then, Jeff sighed, like he was putting up with something he didn't want to deal with. "I get the feeling you need Ruby more than she needs you, Adam." His voice was colder now, more business-like, as he clicked his phone off and reached for an envelope from the desk. "Here's your last check."

Adam took the envelope from Jeff's outstretched hand, his fingers brushing against his uncle's, feeling the disconnection between them. "You're right," Adam said, his voice hollow, strained. "I wrote that text. I . . . I don't know why. But I swear to you, it's not a permanent move." This was the only thing Adam could say to salvage his sanity, to not lose Ruby, or to force Jeff to act.

Jeff didn't respond. Adam could tell he didn't like the words he'd heard. He just sat there, staring at Adam as if he were waiting for him to crack, to reveal something more beneath the shell. But Adam couldn't explain what was happening, couldn't get the words out. It was all a blur: the monkey, the text, the bananas, and the eerie feelings that haunted him even in his waking hours.

"Just give me the weekend," Adam said, his voice barely a whisper. He felt desperate now. "I just need a weekend to get Ruby's things ready. Please."

Jeff didn't say anything for a moment. The air was thick with unspoken tension. Finally, he stood up, walked around the desk, embracing his nephew. "Do what you need to do, Adam. But don't make this harder than it already is for your sister."

Adam nodded, his heart sinking deeper into his chest, a final, heavy weight settling in his bones. "I'll get her things ready," he said, but the words were a lie. Giving Adam two days to fix this monkey business, once and for all.

As he left the office, the door closing behind him with a soft click, Adam couldn't shake the feeling that everything had just slipped even further out of his control. He took a deep breath, grabbed a pen from the counter, and quickly opened the night shift manual where he had left it last. He flipped to the staff directory and wrote Emma's number on his palm.

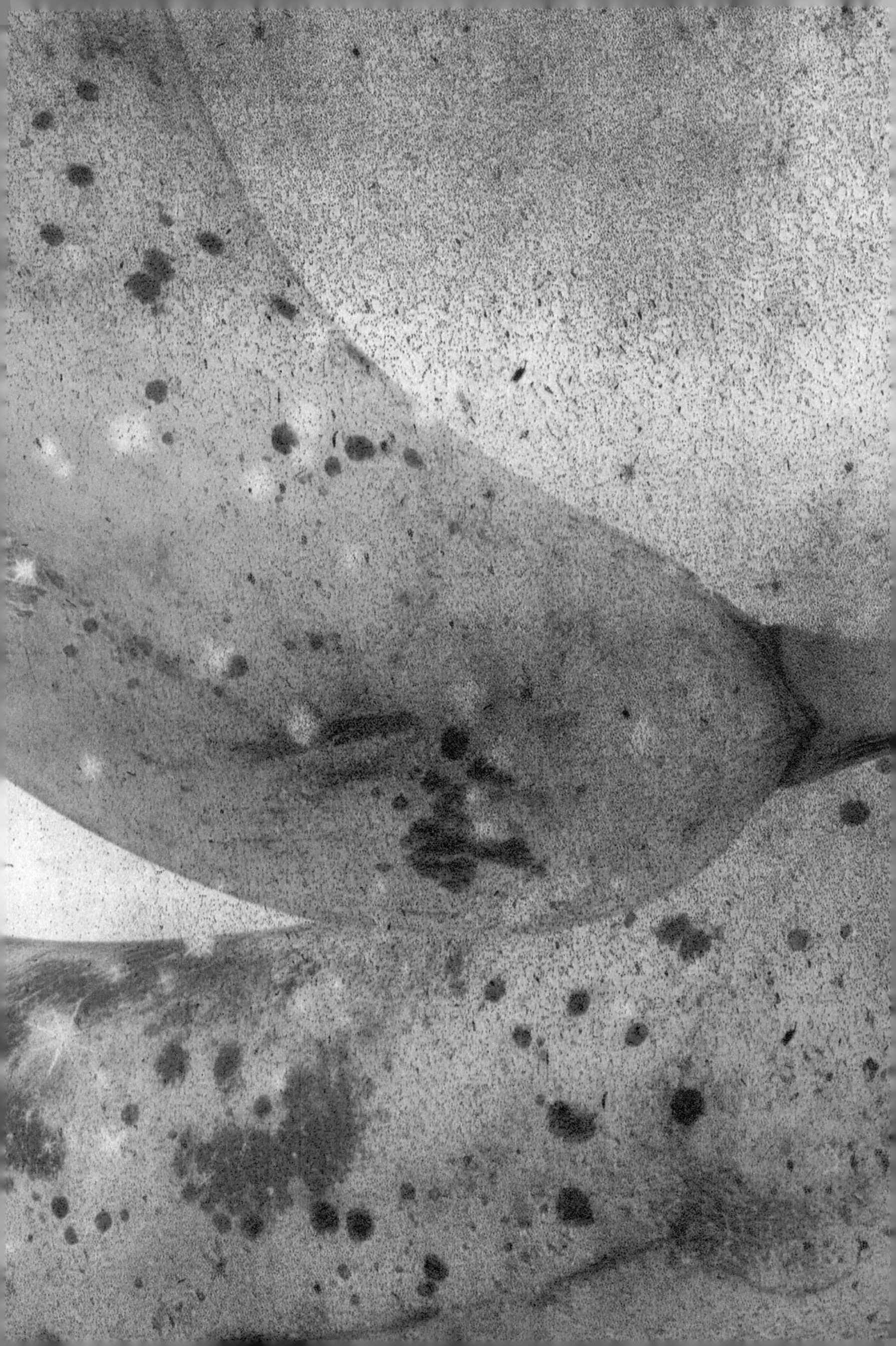

"Sometimes I wonder what is wrong with me"

Coldplay

Chapter 23

Adam came through the door of their childhood home, knowing what awaited him on the other side. An explanation to his sister that he'd failed his first job, in the hopes to prove he can be her legal guardian in less than two weeks. And that he'd been drinking, despite promising to stop at their parents' funeral.

He had wrestled with whether to bring her in on the Dilly bullshit, but he saw no way around it. It was either that he was truly losing his mind, or a monkey from hell was haunting him. Honesty was the best option when it was the only option. He was confident she would believe him because of the desperation in his voice. Even though he'd lied to her using the same tone. Adam opened the door and was immediately assaulted by the smell of ass. As if Satan himself entered their home, squatted, and dropped a cosmic red level deuce in their living room. "Jesus Christ!" Adam shouted, pulling his face back from the threshold of his front door. "Ruby?! You here?!" he shouted, afraid of going in. But no response came. Adam fixed his collar like a cowboy train robber over his nose and walked into his home to be greeted by what seemed to be many pounds of waste splattered all over the walls and fixtures of their house. Photos of their family had shit-caked fingerprints pressed against faces. Immediately, Adam knew what had happened. "Ruby?!" Adam shouted again as he raced to her room. Him not having a phone meant he couldn't track or call her, or even call the police.

Before he left, he went to his father's side of the bed, pulled open the nightstand, and snagged the .45 Smith & Wesson, securely placing it in his satchel. He'd never fired a gun, but this seemed like the only reasonable response to a deranged animal breaking and entering.

He couldn't understand why, but he felt something horrible was about to happen. The same feeling he got on the day of the Diamondbacks game. After packing a few more things he realized he hadn't eaten in quite some time and before his search began for his sister, he needed fuel if he was going to be of any use at all. He went to the filthy kitchen seeking something quick, accessible, and easy. But what he saw made his eyes instantly wet with fear. As he flicked on the kitchen lights, the bananas were waiting. Dozens of unnaturally yellow creatures lining the countertops like a row of crooked grins. The fruit bowl cracked with a brittle snap, tipping sideways as something writhed within. A swarm of blackened bananas began to slither out, each one overripe and splitting at the seams with thick, mucus-y pops. The peels curled back to reveal not fruit but glistening viscera. Knotted veins, veiny hearts, jelly-like clumps of pancreas or brain matter, oozing down the counter like banana slugs.

From beneath the goblin yellow skins, organs slithered free, slick, steaming, purposeful. Livers thudded wetly to the floor. Kidneys dragged themselves by fibrous cords like hellbent snails. Something like a lung peeled open and breathed deep. The bananas kept undressing themselves, revealing their beating and breathing elements.

Adam screamed, a raw, primal, animal noise. His face contorted, every blood vessel in his cheeks and temples bursting into a lattice of terror. He backed into the wall, hyperventilating, mouth wide, unable to close it, unable to unsee. Adam had now fully surrendered both reason and soul to the grotesque logic of the insane.

"So much for Earth,
this life is not what I had planned."

Coldplay

Chapter 23

Chapter 24

The old sofa was replaced with a twin frame, a thin mattress he had purchased from the Goodwill store at the Iron Springs location and a set of purple sheets that seemed almost too vibrant for such a dark room. Yellow pillows, a white side table, and a scattering of stuffed animals completed the scene. Each was meticulously chosen to transform the old den into something that could almost pass for a preteen's sanctuary. The walls, once bare, now had a few hastily framed prints. Generic, smiley faces that didn't quite match the rest of the house's lingering bachelor stench. Jeff stood back, taking in the sight of it, his hands lingering on the doorknob as though searching for something he couldn't quite name.

He had never lived with a child before, but Google had been a patient teacher. What does a pre-teen need to feel at home? Study area, craft corner, string lights, a bulletin board, a small house plant. Each item had been checked off the list, carefully researched, and purchased. The space was perfect, or it should've been. Jeff hadn't felt nervous in his own home in a long time. He liked the feeling. The blinds were pulled open, the light flooded in. He liked that the blinding brightness hid so much. His breathing in the silent house seemed heavier now, deafening to his own ears. He tried to calm his nerves, then the doorbell rang. His niece had arrived.

*"Took a car downtown and took
what they offered me, to set me free."*

Coldplay

Chapter 25

Adam raced to the nearest cell store and purchased a much-needed phone. This was no longer an accessory, but a weapon against the dark arts of monkey bullshit. After all the sales pitches and the back and forth, signing more documents than one does for a baby in a delivery room, Adam headed back to the car and frantically unwrapped his iPhone from its white box, a thing every Apple purchaser loves to do.

With every tear of plastic and cardboard, he felt as if he were paying homage to Steve Jobs, an ancient god gifting humanity fire. Adam tossed the apple stickers and literature on the passenger seat and went through the rigmarole of foreign "hello's" greeting him. He quickly plugged it into the car's charger port, connected it to the invisible cloud for backup, and waited.

A torturous wait. All Adam could do was squeeze his eyes so tightly they hurt, as if that might keep out the intrusive thoughts. Waiting for the new phone, eyes shut tight, jaw clenched, he squeezed his face with his hands. Needing Coldplay, wanting to see that photo again, hoping Ruby was safe. He retrieved Emma's number, the one he'd stolen from the zoo's staff log from his pocket.

Then . . . *Buzz.*

The new phone vibrated. Setup was complete.

Buzz. Again.

A second notification.

But this one . . . this one wasn't from Apple. It wasn't a system message or immediate request for an update.

It was a text message. From a contact labeled Adam Holcomb. Blue letters. iMessage.

From his old phone.

From the godforsaken device that monkey, that thing, had run off with.

His pulse skipped. Skin prickled. Every hair on his body stood like it was listening. *There is no goddamn way,* he thought. *No way that chimp, or anything else, has this new number.*

And yet . . .

His thumb hovered over the message, twitching, hesitant, like it knew what opening it meant. As if the screen were Pandora's box, pulsing with something wrong. Something loose.

But curiosity always wins. Always.

He clicked. Dragged. The screen glowed.

And there it was.

One text. One emoji. A fucking banana.

Sent from a phone no one should have. From something that should not be able to text. From . . . Dilly, the chimpanzee from the seventh circle of hell.

And in the quiet dark of the car, the screen hummed with digital innocence. But Adam's blood froze.

Beneath the absurdity of the banana text, he felt the cold edge of an invitation. A threat pressing in from the other side.

*"Cause my head just aches when I think of the things
that I shouldn't have done"*

Coldplay

Emma sat against her apartment wall, staring at memories that never were. The spider peel's webbing still draped her trashy apartment like smoke, but she no longer gave a shit. Between emotional breakdowns and wiping her snot on her sleeve, she could hear the spider peel tapping the glass, trying to get her attention. Every time she looked over at the thing, it was staring at her. She'd never felt guilt with such weight before in her short life. It settled behind her eyes and beneath her ribs. Guilt had found her hiding from it, the way the Grim Reaper finds his victims. She'd been ignoring the whispers, but now it was screaming. A constant question that wouldn't stop asking, *What if you had waited? What if you had stayed with him? What if you had let it live?* Emma stared at the image of her ex-husband lifting the child-who-never-was into the air. What was years ago felt present. She left him not because she stopped loving him, but because she couldn't bear the look in his eyes that didn't accuse but still knew. She wasn't ready for a child, and he was. His gentleness only magnified the shame after the fact. And that house, that life, that man, all of it spoke too loudly.

So, she ran.

But guilt is not geographical. It travels like ghosts do, with no borders or respect for the boundaries of man. Phantoms don't consider our new starting points, or resolutions. The guilt had curled itself around her bones like cancer, and pressed itself into the shape of her shadow. It turned mirrors into enemies. It made the sound of a child crying in another aisle at the store feel like thunder in her chest. She could still hear her baby weep from within her gut, like Abel's blood in the dirt.

Her new life away from him, away from the child, didn't change her. Only her surroundings did.

She had decided. One moment. One choice. And though the world said it was over, her body had healed, and the clinic had closed the file. In every way possible, her life had moved on.

But her soul didn't.

Guilt became her architecture, building invisible walls within her fragile frame. Orchestrations of memories lined her gut with hallways and arches. This was what kept her awake, her demon, who came and sat by her bedside. Whispering new doctrines and gospels into her ear like the devil in the garden.

It's not that she didn't believe in forgiveness, but she wasn't sure she was allowed to ask for it, and now, under the rotting peels of bananas she felt pressured to face the architect.

Emma stood and began to take down each frame and gently lay them on her couch. As if they were priceless artifacts. But as she was stirring up her destroyed memories, her phone buzzed. It was Jeff from the zoo, texting something. Through her blurry, wet eyes, she couldn't make out the words quite yet, but she could see it was important as everything was in all caps. Then she read the words,

EMMA, COME IN ASAP!
EMERGENCY!
WE NEED SUPPORT! MORE
ANIMAL FATALITIES!

Subject: Urgent Request: Transfer of Last Chimpanzee from Closing Sanctuary

I'm sorry it had to come to this, but this is where it ends. We will not be accepting the return of the chimpanzee, Daffodil.

My strongest recommendation? Leave the facility. Or better yet, find some other poor soul to offload that nightmare onto.

Consider this your final warning.

Nancy Hesson

"Come on rage with me"

Coldplay

Chapter 27

Lena, the zoo receptionist, worked Sunday through Thursday, and without fail unlocked the side gate at 6:00 a.m. sharp. She hadn't missed an unlock in over twenty years. She was the longest living primate at the zoo, and has no plans to retire. This job has been her dream, and she wouldn't exchange it for the world. The keys jingled, the air smelled of wet concrete and eucalyptus, and the zoo sat, anticipating another day. But this morning, Lena noticed something wasn't quite right.

There were no birdsongs. In fact, there were no animal sounds whatsoever.

She paused at the entrance. The aviary on the western end, which usually pulsed with whistles and morning chatter, was dead silent.

Her boots crunched over the gravel as she stepped onto the path. That's where she saw it.

One white cockatoo, sprawled on the walkway like it had fallen mid-flight . . . but it hadn't. The wings were rounded out, like an angel. The neck twisted. No blood, no marks, except for a dark bruise beneath the beak. Like fingers.

Lena blinked and took another step.

The Red Eclectus Parrot lay six feet ahead in the same manner. Stiff. Sprawled wings. Face down. Body up. Neck wrong.

She looked up. The wire mesh of the aviary loomed to her right, wide open. Not cut. Not broken. Just . . . unlatched.

That's when the smell hit her.

Metallic. Feathery. Soil. Shit.

A sick dread bloomed in her chest, making it hard to breathe, her heart hammering wildly. She walked faster now, then slower, as she saw the line.

Six. Seven. Eight. They were spaced evenly down the path, each bird placed, not tossed. Not dropped. Fucking placed. A line of dead beauties, yellow, red, green, blue. Their colors looked obscene on the cold gray path.

He was still there. The predator. The chimpanzee. He was out of his medical enclosure, standing tall at the end of the path . . . watching her. His chin was high, and his body was statuesque. His fur was streaked with feathers and bits of blood, but his face was calm. Strangely calm. Not panting. Not frantic. Serene. Almost human. As if getting seen was the purpose all along.

In one hand, Lena could see what looked like a phone, and in his other hand, what had to be the zoo's last parrot. Colorful, alive, and trembling in its hands like a fresh infant.

Lena couldn't move, couldn't breathe, couldn't look away.

The chimp's fingers flexed. Slowly and deliberately. The tropical bird let out one tiny squeak. Then silence. Lena watched as it popped into his hands. A small, colorful explosion that burst from its grip.

He turned from her gaze, walked forward with slow, swaying steps, and placed the final bird on the path, like the last word in a sentence.

Then he looked at Lena again. Tilting his head. Curious and waiting. Like he had made something for her.

Lena bolted for the zoo office. She could hear the animal behind her sprinting and moaning. She looked over her shoulder at the dark figure that was now running on two legs. As her hand met the door knob, she felt fingers like iron wrench her ponytail. She screamed as her body snapped backward, skull cracking against the concrete. The office lights spun above her, then vanished. Above the ringing in her ears came a sound so unnatural it seemed to warp the air around it . . . laughter.

"The judgment of this court is we need more guns
Stop
Everything's gone so crazy"

Coldplay

Every dead bird had its wings fanned out like they were in flight. Soaring upon the dust from which they came. The entire path of the small zoo was lined with differing forms and species of every bird under their care. Each one, deceased. From the Violetear Hummingbird to the Harpy Eagle. Every six feet, from the entrance to the exit, peacocks, turkey vultures, hens and night owls, all dead.

Emma walked through the corpses. Surprisingly, she found she wasn't as bothered by the sight of dead birds because they distracted her from other dead things. A handful of other staff were there, including the local Prescott Police. It was obvious to every single zoo crew member that this was a premeditated, fucking annihilation. But, after Emma's last twenty-four hours, she wasn't so sure anymore what was fiction and what was real.

She made her way to Jeff, who was talking to the officers. One was taking photos with his phone and the other was scratching his brow with a notebook. You could tell they were out of their depth as detectives, let alone bird murderers. Emma didn't want to alert Jeff that she was behind him as she tried to eavesdrop on what had been discovered so far, and then she heard it.

"Cardiac rupture."

Each bird's body had a monster's hands around it with such dominion, each of their hearts had popped in their chest. Someone or something had squeezed them one by one. Emma could only imagine the shrieking sounds of their cries, their wings fluttering heavily against their predator's hands in a desperate attempt to escape. Her empathy forced her to grip herself, feeling her own beating heart, sensing her eyes grow red. When things died now, she felt herself shed a new skin. As if she also wished to become new at the sight of it. She looked back at the bird corpses, studying their postures, seeing patches of red skin and disheveled feathers from where the attacker detonated them. Even some of their beaks were snapped in half, while others had their beaks completely torn from their small faces.

"I see security cameras; have you checked the footage?" The officer asked, pointing with his pen. "We do, but our system just recently had a bit of an accident," Jeff said with a sigh.

"Accident?"

"Yeah, one of our team members spilled some liquid on it. Frying the laptop."

"Okay, do you have a night shift or a guard of some kind?" the officer asked, as he scribbled.

"We did. He was recently let go."

"He was recently let go?"

"Yes, does that matter?"

"That depends, was the termination on good terms?"

"Is a termination ever on good terms?" Jeff replied, with a bitter edge.

"What I mean is, do we have a possible motive because of a disgruntled employee?" the officer asked.

"No, no, not with Adam. He's my nephew, we're on good terms. He understood completely." Emma couldn't help overhearing while she raised a brow.

"Can I ask why he was let go?" the officer asked again, his tone changing the interview into an investigation.

"We had an incident of negligence, resulting in some animal deaths—" The minute Jeff said it out loud, he saw the officer's conclusions fall into place. Jeff could see the police officer's body language change, as he came closer and flipped another page in his notebook. "We had some older Japanese tortoises that passed in the night, three of them, due to a food and water machine outage."

"Cortez!" the officer yelled, calling his partner over. "When did your cameras stop working?"

"Just the other night."

"And who was on shift during the accident?" Before Jeff could answer, he could feel his gut expand as if it was filling with concrete. "Adam." He said hesitantly.

"Can I get Adam's number and address?"

"Yes," Jeff said with tragic surrender in his tone, pulling his phone from his pocket.

"We'll also need Lena's number and home address. We'll let you know once we find her."

"Please do!" Jeff said nervously. "She hasn't missed a day of work the entire time I've been here."

"And just to double check, you're sure she was here this morning?"

"Her key was still in the front gate, something she's never done before."

"Okay, Mr. Harrison, we'll let you know what we find," the officers concluded, shaking Jeff's hand.

Emma stood a few feet away listening confused, and disturbed. The feeling of her phone buzzing in her pocket pulled her out of the moment. It was a text . . . from Adam.

Emma texted back a question mark, clearly confused by the childish message.

Then another text came through:

?

She would've had your eyes

"I'm ready for the change."

Coldplay

Chapter 29

As Adam was driving to the zoo, his new phone, with a new number, was being spammed by the chimpanzee under label of his own name. Adam reading texts from Adam. As if his self, his doppelgänger was trying to break through the screen. A constant barrage of dings and buzzes from Dilly, bananas filling his notification screen. Adam had fully settled into the reality that whatever was happening had to be supernatural, or alien, or the most elaborate hoax just to fuck with him. But he knew it wasn't the latter, as his life was just too broken to fuck with.

As he sat at a stoplight, his eyes shifted down to his fingers and thumbs, which gripped the steering wheel. He judged himself for allowing his fingernails to grow so long, even distracted by how filthy his hands were, unable to remember the last time he'd showered. But the longer he stared, the more he noticed something. On his thumb was a hangnail, but something about it was off. Inhuman even. His hangnail resembled those pale-yellow banana strings that you peel off the fruit before eating. Adam scratched at it, tapping it to satisfy his curiosity. He pinched it between his fingers and tugged. First slowly, then hard. It gave resistance, not like natural plant fiber, more like something . . . embedded. He pulled harder.

His skin moved.

Not just on the surface, but deeper within him. The phloem bundle wasn't just resting or attached to him. It was him. A banana thread was sewn through dermis and nerve and flesh. His breath hitched. He yanked again. A pink strip unfurled from his thumb like a wet skin ribbon. Flesh continued with it. Creating long red lines. Crimson rivers where flesh should be. Adam yelped at the sharp sting of pain. Another pull, he was too compelled to stop. Too fearful to leave it. Another strip. Another red river. And beneath his skin, it only seemed to be muscle met with banana pulp.

A honk from a car behind him tore Adam away from his unraveling, shocking him back to reality. He'd half expected to see his thumb back to normal, hoping it was just another vision or dream from hell. But it wasn't. Adam's thumb was bleeding as banana threads were peeled down his hand and up his wrist.

He couldn't tell if his whole body was now skin becoming fruit. As pale yellow meat, soft and strung together by trembling, fruity threads, rotted sweetly from inside of himself.

Fuck me, Adam thought to himself.

"I've got to get out of this hole"

Coldplay

Jeff's old, yappy Bichon Frise, Precious, danced around Ruby's legs. The white hair around its mouth had yellowed. The color around its eyes was stained with brownish rings. Ruby never really liked the dumb dog. But now it was to be her new roommate, so she was going to make the best of it.

Ruby unpacked slowly, dragging each folded shirt from the duffel like she was exhuming pieces of someone else's life. The room Jeff gave her was coated in soft pastels and Pinterest femininity. Faux peonies, sequin pillows, wall decals that read, "You are enough." She hated them as she always preferred posters of Edward Scissorhands more than Edward Cullen.

Ruby tried to convince herself that this could be a long stay but hated herself for thinking about it. Halfway through, she aborted the whole process and let her clothes collapse into a heap at the foot of the bed. The house felt heavy . . . and odd. Jeff was handling an emergency at the zoo. An escaped bird, some bleeding lemur, who knew. But that meant she was in his house alone.

She'd been here hundreds of times before with her parents, but since their passing, she hadn't been back. Without them here with her, the house felt lifeless, strange even. It felt like a museum to something that died but hadn't been buried. She opened the fridge. Deli meat and light beer. *Food for the gods*, she thought. The drawers? Empty, except for some bent plastic utensils and a kitchen knife. One frying pan in a cupboard that echoed. The dining room table was buried in unopened mail, animal anatomy charts, wildlife permits, and magazines with gorillas on the covers. Ruby thumbed through a stack of zoological paperwork with the flat interest of someone flipping through obituaries.

Curiosity piqued, she and Precious wandered deeper.

Jeff's room was locked, which Ruby found odd, as there was no one in his room and the door handle could only be locked from the outside. And not with a push button, but an actual key. She didn't think too much about it until she noticed her bedroom door. Not only could it be locked from the outside, but it also had a separate bolt lock at the top of the door for an entirely separate key.

"The cuck?" she whispered, gliding her fingers over the cool metal.

She pulled out her phone and snapped a picture. Not because she knew what to do with it, but because something inside her whispered she'd want proof of this later. She checked her ringer, on. Still no missed calls. No voicemails. Just a wall of silence from Adam.

Annoyed. Then worried. Then . . . whatever. She fired off another text.

It was the fiftieth she'd sent since Adam's horrific prank of covering their house in shit. All she could do was chalk it up to mental instability. And then, the ellipsis. Typing.

She plopped on the bed, a wave of relief flooding her as she sank into the musty fabric.

Her face went still.

We need to talk about mommy and daddy

call me loser, you owe me a big ol chubby apology. Im at jeffs place

Another text.

Check the closet

The sentence was a blade to the gut. She blinked hard. Looked up. The closet stood in the corner like it had been watching her this whole time. Waiting. Hungry. Wrong.

She sent another text off.

Adam, call me NOW

She stood and walked to the closet as if pulled. The hinges moaned like an old witch. There was nothing inside. A few wire hangers, a sickly stretch of seventies shag carpet. But the air inside felt different. Cooler. A draft? She ran her hand along the back wall. Cheap paneling. Her fingers brushed something, a hole. Not some ancient and forgotten nail hole. This was hidden. This was intentional.

Her mouth flooded with the sour warmth of rising bile. Her skin crawled as if something beneath it wanted out.

And then her phone buzzed. Precious barked a few yips, as if sensing something wasn't right in the world.

One new message.

This isn't Adam.

"And if you were to ask me
After all that we've been through
'Still believe in magic?'
Oh, yes, I do"

Coldplay

Chapter 30

Chapter 31

Emma sat in the dim zoo office, gnawing her nails down to raw edges. Her hands trembled, not from the blasting AC unit, but from anxiety. A cigarette would've taken the edge off, but she'd left them at home. And going back there? Not a chance. The house reeked of something worse than leftover Arby's and smoke. It reeked of terror. And she was far too afraid to go back, and far too terrified to prolong her stay at the zoo which was quickly becoming something closer to a morgue.

Jeff had gathered the entire staff to deliver the verdict: The zoo was shutting down indefinitely. Five days' paid leave. After that, nothing. No answers. No plan. Just silence and the slow unraveling of whatever normal life Emma thought she had left.

She pulled out her phone, her thumb hovering over the glowing screen like she was searching for an exit. Maybe, if she typed in the right words, she'd get clarity, or at least confirm that she wasn't losing her mind. "Dead animals and bananas." "Banana spiders and lost memories fucked up." Nothing. Nothing but weird images of yellow bugs and the random dude wiener. Useless.

As she opened the back-office door, hoping to slip out before Jeff cornered her again, someone was already there: Adam.

"Adam?!" she whisper-hissed, pushing him further out than in.

"Emma! Just the person I needed to see," he said, breathless with relief.

"Now's really not a good time," she said, shoving past him.

"Wait, please. I've got no one else. My little sister might be in trouble." Adam said, grabbing her arm.

Emma yanked her arm free. "Seriously, that sucks for you. But I've got my own weird banana shit to deal with."

"Wait, bananas?" Adam said, slowing his pace to keep up with Emma as she marched to her car. "Are you just saying that, or are you dealing with actual banana weird shit?"

She turned slowly, narrowing her eyes like she was trying to spot the wires of a hidden camera. "Are you fucking with me?"

"I wish," he said. Adam sighed, as if getting ready to uncage everything within him. "I know that I can't stop having nightmares about that stupid fruit. I know that my sister is missing, and my house is filled with monkey feces. I know my uncle is not on my side and a is total two-faced piece of shit. I know that I'm losing my goddamn mind, because that fucking chimpanzee in the zoo stole my phone and I'm pretty sure it won't stop texting me and it's completely fucking me up!" Adam said loudly, pulling his phone from his pocket and showing Emma his text messages.

He pulled out his phone, his fingers shaking. The screen lit up with thousands of unread messages . . . all banana emojis. Emma scrolled in stunned silence, her finger gliding like a match being struck. The absurdity. The horror. It all blurred together.

"Jesus Christ," she whispered.

"Emma, please listen to me. I have no one else in my life, and Daffodil, that new chimpanzee . . . something is very wrong with that animal. My life has only started to come apart since coming to this fucking zoo."

Emma looked at him. Really looked at him for the first time. He was drenched in sweat, eyes bloodshot, breathing like he'd been chased. And yet, it all made an eerie kind of sense. Two strangers, each suffocating in the same impossible story. Two aliens from different planets, speaking the same broken language.

She exhaled. Slowly and deliberately.

"You got a cigarette?" she asked, her shoulders finally dropping.

Adam nodded. "Yeah. Want one?"

She nodded back.

"Wait," she said, lighting the cigarette in her mouth, "so have you texted the monkey back?"

Part 2

Chapter 31

Chapter 32

In 1888, a wealthy benefactor only known as Conklin fancied himself an English occultist, poet, and mountaineer. He enlisted his assistant, Jake Cook, to voyage to the Congo in search of "exotic creatures for his collection."

He returned not with pelts, feathers, or tusks . . . but with a single chimpanzee that the locals call Bisu-Bisu, translated, "It Sees Both Ways." Only, Bisu-Bisu wasn't . . . normal.

Mr. Cook had to smuggle the first known chimpanzee into the American South, under the claim it was for medical purposes and would advance human flourishing. An English booklet written at this time by journalist Henry S. Fuller, titled, *The Chimpanzee of Central Park* sheds light on the situation by saying, "Some men bring snakes in jars. Conklin brought something that walked like a boy and wept like a widow."

Conklin was smitten with his findings and eagerly established the animal with the director of the Zoological Collection at The Arsenal in Central Park, making Bisu-Bisu a unique specimen for study while simultaneously offering an amazing attraction for The Arsenal's public. Conklin learned pretty much right away that Bisu-Bisu wasn't like other beasts. He was more curious and conscious. Within months, the ape was eating with a knife and fork, painting with watercolors and practicing his phonics. But that's where simplicity ends. Whispers note that Conklin taught the beast more than how to grind Prussian blue or crack oyster shells. He crossed a line no man should. He offered books that should've stayed locked away. They say he fed the animal the infernal craft, and it learned. Not like a pet, but like a pupil. Like something watching from the dark, waiting to turn the spell back on its master.

Within a year's time, the chimpanzee became increasingly frustrated and began to refuse to eat. It would scratch words into wood, some saying they could hear it mimic the voices of the dead. Depending on what literature you read, there are claims that its eyes grew human-shaped, developing white around the yellow iris. Locals swore they heard the beast crying in Latin during one of Conklin's "special lessons." One visitor to The Arsenal said the chimp whispered secrets about his adulterous wife.

Local papers at the time became a firestorm of fear and superstitious rage. Headlines reading, "Conklin: The Man Who Brought the Devil in a Cage." Asking questions like, "Divine punishment or gift? Depends on who you ask."

Conklin didn't help the matter by responding with supernatural flair, "I did not bring him here. I answered his call. He is not from any jungle, but from a place beneath reason, where God buried the first lie."

When a drought scorched the land in 1890, Conklin's ape was blamed, and the phrase "HELL WANTS IT BACK" was carved into the front gate of his New York home.

After some time, the county tried to seize and destroy the creature, but by the time they stormed Conklin's property, both Conklin and the chimpanzee had vanished. Conklin's house was filled with hundreds of pages of the creature's gibberish writings and paintings. None legible, all circular and looping into eyes and spirals. Thousands of rotten banana peels plagued the house with fruit flies and a dewy, moldy stench. The chimpanzee was never seen again.

In one burned journal page, Crowley allegedly wrote:

3 July, 1890, New York, New York

The air is stifling, thick with the incessant rasp of horse flies. He mimics them now. I can hear him in the other room, singing and moaning.

I must record this with utmost clarity, if only to exorcise what remains of my reason.

I ought never to have removed him from the jungle. I ought never to have taught him unhallowed arts. At the time, I believed him to be a specimen, rare, yes, but nonetheless part of the natural order. I was grievously mistaken.

He is no creature of God's common earth. He is a distortion. A specter encased in flesh. A trespasser on life.

The Congolese would not name him outright, save in hushed tones. They called him Bisu-Bisu—he who sees in both directions. My assumptions can only be that they feared he could gaze backward into the dead and forward into what ought never come to pass. I, of course, dismissed this as tribal superstition. Fool that I was.

He is male, yes, and appears in the form of a chimpanzee—but in his bearing, in his eyes, in the silence that gathers around him like smoke, there is something unfathomably ancient. He speaks now. Not in words precisely, but in borrowed voices. Last night he uttered my brother's name in an inflection I have not heard since he hung himself.

He does not eat. He does not sleep. He waits. And the house is not large enough to contain him anymore.

I observed him by lamplight not an hour ago, standing upright by the window. The way a prophet looks over the lost. He frightens me. I believe now, with all that is left of my heart, that I did not retrieve him. I released him.

This is not a precautionary note. This is a confession of guilt. He feeds from it. I shouldn't have educated in the ways of Maleficium, this is the cross upon my shoulders.

I am sorry.
He is already among us all.

"Bisu–Bisu by the fire"

"I don't want to follow Death and all of his friends"

Coldplay

Chapter 32

Chapter 33

Once the police officers were done photographing the dead birds along the path, Jeff and his team began to carefully pick them up and place them into different sized bags. When animals die at a zoo, there are specific protocols for handling and transporting the remains, and that often includes placing the animal in specially designated body bags or containment units. It's not your average throw your dead Labrador Retriever in a street bin styled disposal. There's labeling, documentation, refrigeration, cremation, and bio security measures. Let alone the paperwork for removal of government funding and deceasement.

Jeff knew the kind of work it would take to bag and seal over forty-five different specimens and the logistics only intensified his pre-existing rage. The entire staff was at work, crying and carefully doing their due diligence to care for the dead. Jeff's back ached as he was bending over, so he was relieved when his phone buzzed in his pocket.

A text from Adam.

But what he saw he could never have prepared for. The blue glow went red. They were photos of Lena. Bloodied. Purple. Swollen. Animalistic. Then a pin dropped in the text chat. The monkey with Adam's phone was playing a game of Catch Me If You Can, and Jeff had no idea he was the mouse.

Jeff pushed the toothpick to the other side of his mouth and clicked the pin. The geographical location was a hundred yards away. He waved the phone around himself to help pinpoint his destination, the way a treasure hunter might with a compass. Then he marched, which soon turned into a sprint. Jeff shouted at some of the nearby staff as he picked up speed, "Get those police back here and have them meet me by the east end!"

He ran past the maintenance shed, down near the dry ravine where the old electric fencing gave out years ago. Nobody went there, not anymore. His mind darted in a thousand ways to deny that this could be the work of his nephew. The same nephew who peed in his pool and loved to walk his dogs as a child. But grief has a way of mutating you. Dread bloomed in his gut, a mushroom cloud of fear.

For the animals.

For Lena.

For Adam.

For himself.

He crested the desert hill and froze. Ice riveted through his veins in the Arizona heat.

There she was.

Lena was dead.

Splayed on her back like a sacrifice. Not entirely different from the birds. A circle of offerings surrounded her like a Painted Bunting bird. Hundreds of rotten banana peels, shiny garbage, feathers, the snatched bird beaks, her broken flashlight, a sock, and more dead zoo animals. Her staff badge lay on her exposed chest like a morgue tag. Whoever did this wanted the identification to be clear.

Jeff stumbled toward his old friend, knees going weak. His voice cracked, useless. "Lena . . ."

The red Arizona dirt around her body was stamped with large handprints. Like molded clay, the killer was an artist. Her blood and plasma were its watercolors. All of it, deliberate. Illegible words were written around her head in the painterly mud.

Her mouth was open, as if forced. The jaw was clearly broken, wide and disjointed. Something had defecated on her face, but it felt reverent, like a communion offering.

Then his phone buzzed in his hand.

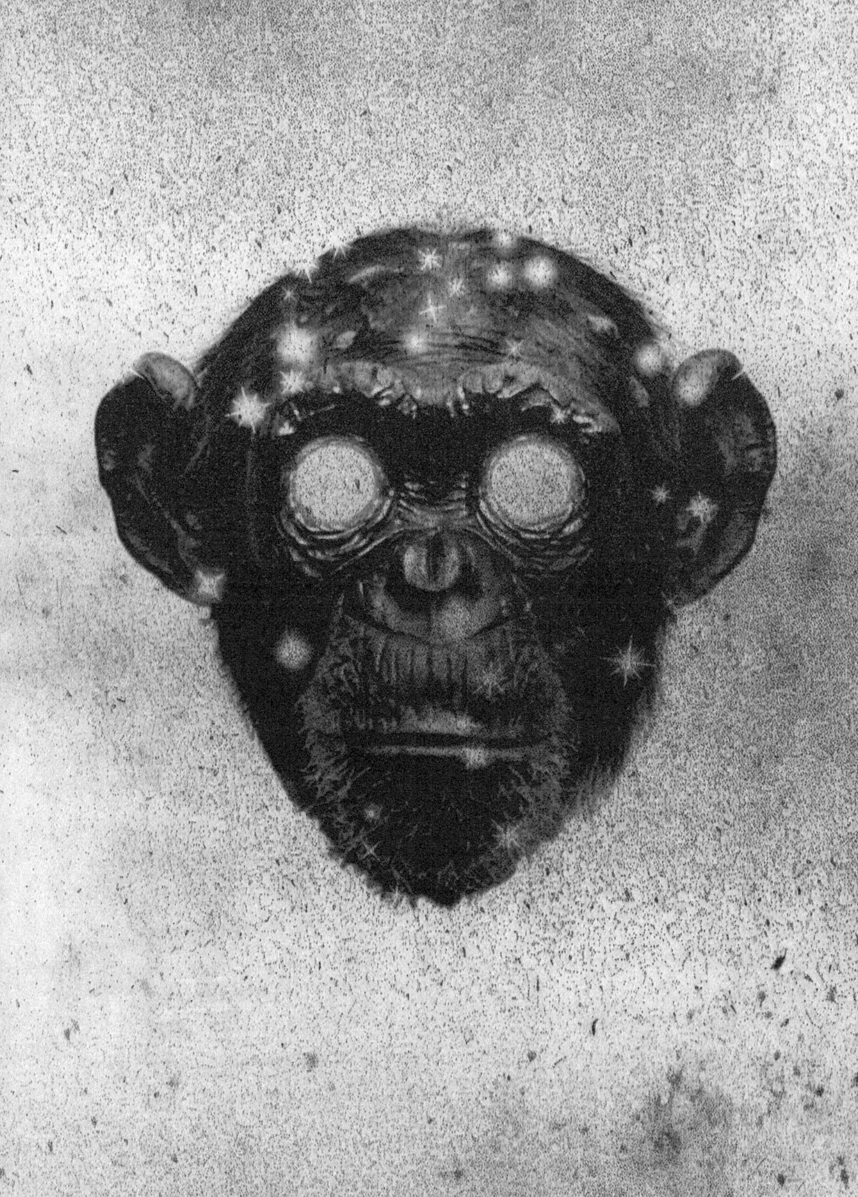

" . . . spread it all around"

Coldplay

Chapter 33

Chapter 34

Brenda glanced at her phone. It was Adam.

She hadn't heard from him in days, not since the last session, the one that left her uneasy. The sudden message made her stomach tighten. She opened it immediately.

No words. Just a photo.

Adam, what am I looking at?

A reply came almost instantly.

Do you see it? Do you see what I've done?

Her fingers hovered. She stared at the screen.

See what, exactly?

A pause.

She felt her throat tighten.

Why is it so hard for the many eyed giants to watch the world rot but never see their own fingers dripping red?

Adam, why don't we schedule a session and talk this through?

Silence.

Brenda looked away from the phone, wondering if he knew. Wondering if he knew she advised against his request for guardianship?

Does he know? Impossible.

She stared back at the screen, guilt and fear flooding through her.

Another banana emoji.

Then another.

Then another.

Then another.

Then another.

Then five more.

The phone buzzed harder as rows of bananas flooded in, faster and faster, covering the screen, smothering the chat window in yellow.

Thirty. Fifty. Seventy.

The screen trembled in her hand. The heat from the phone rose quickly, burning against her skin.

Cracks splintered across the glass. Thin lines at first. Then a sudden snap. The screen shattered with a sharp *pop!* She yelped, dropping it to the floor.

The phone hit hard, face up, still buzzing, still pulsing with bananas.

And though she was alone, from somewhere in the room, she felt as if something was with her. A presence closer than her own breath. Her nose was filled with the smell of feces and wildness, forcing her to cover her face and eyes to water.

Her phone wouldn't stop buzzing. And then, a final text. A photo. *The photo.* For the first time, another pair of human eyes has seen what was to always remain hidden.

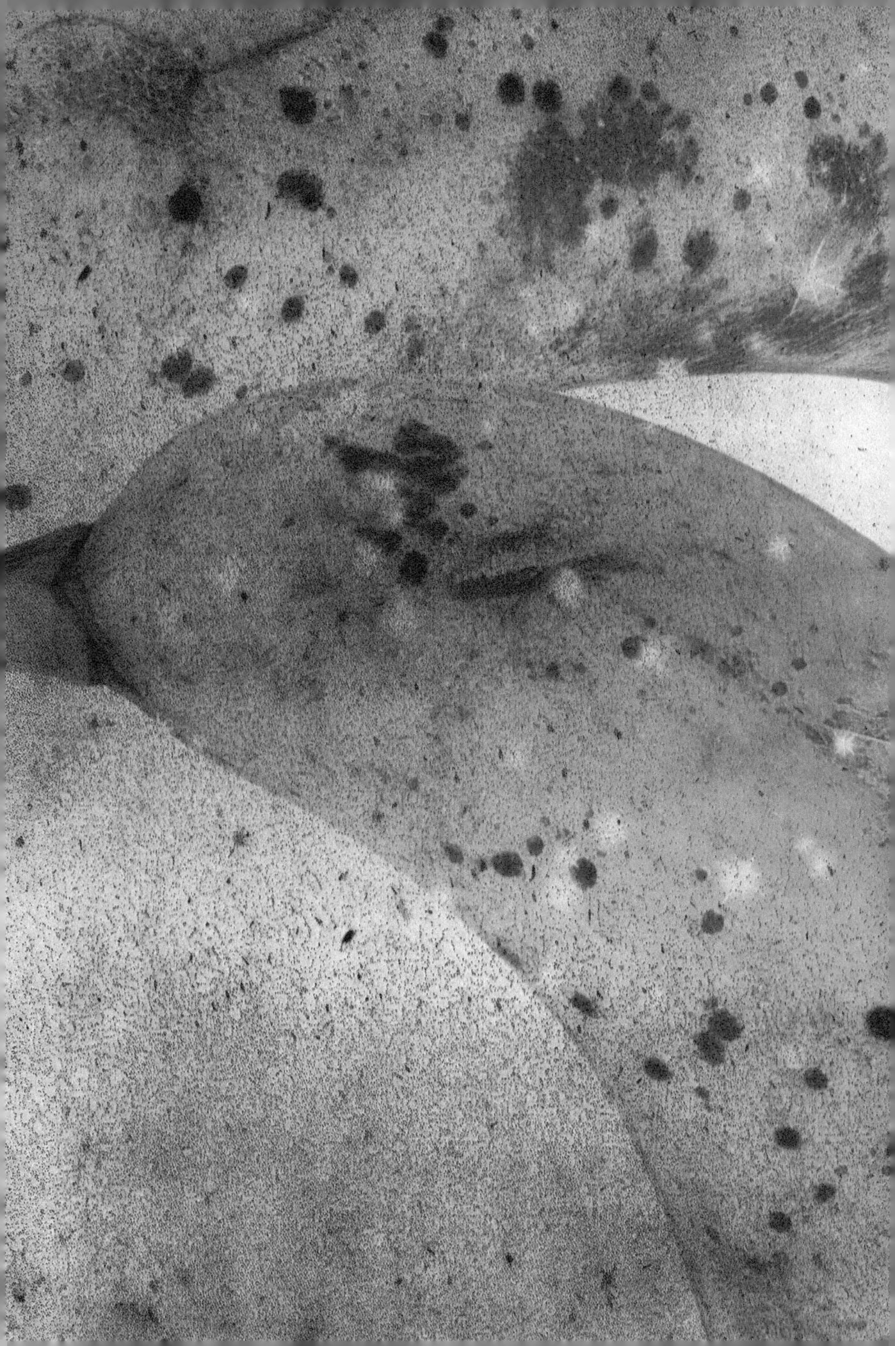

"Do you wanna talk about it?
Oh, you're gonna get it right sometime
Is there something missing?
Is nobody listening?"

Coldplay

Chapter 34

Chapter 35

"I'm texting your uncle for Ruby's number now," Emma muttered, her thumbs flying across the screen as they sat in her Jeep Wagoneer. The air inside was thick with the sour tang of old fries and incense residue. Adam shifted uncomfortably in his seat, glancing around the mobile disaster zone. The floor was buried under layers of trash, crumpled clothes, gas station snacks, and fast-food wrappers hardened like ancient scrolls. It smelled like menthol, patchouli, and despair.

The rearview mirror was completely eclipsed by a tangle of backstage passes, rusted keychains, and peace sign necklaces that clinked together like wind chimes from a forgotten era. There was no glove compartment, just a gaping cavity revealing part of the vehicle's internal anatomy, like a body with its chest cracked open.

"Uh … do you live in here?" Adam asked, squinting.

"I do now."

"What do you mean?"

"I mean my apartment was overtaken by banana bugs. And possibly Satan. So, I'm going to sleep in Wal-Mart parking lots or something for now while I pray for dawn."

Adam blinked. "Wait, by Satan? By banana—"

His words were chopped in half by another buzz from her phone. "He didn't give me Ruby's number, but he's asking where you're at." Emma leaned back in her seat. "Can I have another cigarette?" she asked, rolling down her window. Adam handed her the half empty pack, then dug his nails into his scalp, trying to scratch out a solution. He knew he looked deranged as he rubbed his face and pulled up his hair, as if he thought he could tunnel through his forehead into the brain matter for better ideas.

"Didn't you ever do an iCloud backup?" Emma asked, squinting at her phone. "Shouldn't her number be in there?"

"Yeah, but I never updated it. All I have is her old number, from months ago." Adam's voice sounded like a deflated tire.

Another buzz on Emma's phone. Emma glanced at the screen and went stiff. It was from Jeff.

AVOID ADAM. DANGEROUS.

No other context.

Her fingers froze over the message. Her breath caught. A thousand survival instincts screamed at her. She barely knew this guy. What if Jeff, her boss, was right? What if she'd just crawled out of one nightmare and into another? Emma grew uncomfortable in the car. Even though the sky was falling in her own life, his story did sound utterly insane. *iPhone wielding chimps?* she thought. But then again, so were banana spiders. Emma peered out of the corner of her eyes. She couldn't be sure, but it looked like he had an outline of a pistol in the waistband of his pants.

"Hey, what about DMs?" Adam blurted, realizing the obvious, and breaking the silence with a flicker of hope.

Emma nodded, too fast, "Yeah. Yeah. Can you check?"

"Yes!" Adam's fingers fumbled across the screen. "Shit, it's making me log in. I don't know my fucking password."

"Reset it," she exhaled sharply, her grip tightening on the steering wheel. "Listen, dude, I need some kind of proof that this monkey thing is real. I'm kind of in a fragile state, and I need a reality check a bit here. I'm a little shaken up. What can you do to prove to me that Dilly is behind this all?"

Adam was caught off guard but understood. "Well ..." he said, quickly realizing there wasn't much proof to offer. His mind went through the photos, which he had none of. Zero video, either of his own or the zoo's. The texts wouldn't hold up in court, and there was nothing at his house besides a living room full of shit. Then it hit him. "There's one way to prove it," he said slowly. "We must find Dilly. In the flesh."

Emma narrowed her eyes. "What about Ruby?"

"Text my uncle. Just ask if she's there. If she's safe. If she is . . . we've got breathing room." Adam had no other option but to believe the best about his uncle. Leaving Ruby in his care seemed like the wisest plan he's had yet.

"Why would he tell me about her? I have nothing to do with her!" Emma asked, logic cockblocking certain movements of her mind.

"Just find a way to phrase it and see if you can get an answer from him!" Emma stared at him for a beat too long. Her thumb hovered over the electric keyboard. Adam sensed her hesitation, reached across the Jeep's center console and grabbed her hand firmly, but not forcefully.

"Please, Emma. You have to trust me."

She looked down at his hand, at the long scrapes that spanned the length of it, the disfiguration of his thumb, the way he was shaking.

Then she moved up to his eyes.

They were terrified.

And that terrified her more than anything.

"If sweet death should ever come for me"

Coldplay

Ruby sat on her bed, discerning the situation. Her thoughts were flying like a bat into the night. *This doesn't mean my uncle, my mother's brother, is a friggen pedo, right? The hole was left over when he moved in years ago. My uncle has always been cool with me . . . On the other hand, my uncle has always been cool with me.*

From her bag, she pulled a frame of her family from their day at Universal Studios Hollywood, months before the accident. Fingers glazed over the image as she remembered what her mother told her, *"I'm not raising you to fold. Fuck laundry, fuck fear."* Her mother always wanted to make sure she wasn't raising no bitch. Ruby was smiling as the tears came, remembering how her mother would introduce her as *"the woman who will one day either rule the world, or ruin it.*" Ruby couldn't help but feel she was letting her down, that from vision beyond this life, she was disappointed that she was sitting here afraid. Angry. A victim.

Ruby stormed out of the room to retrieve the knife from the kitchen. She pulled it from the drawer, the way Arthur jerked his sword from the stone. She gripped the kitchen knife like it was the only real thing in the world, which, at that moment, it was. It was literally the only kitchen knife in the house. She liked the weight of the knife. It grounded her, steadied her breath as she leaned in front of the closet wall again. The peephole stared back at her like a pupil in the wall.

She pressed the blade into the drywall and began to carve. Beneath her, Precious stood guard, curiously watching and getting snowed upon by the drywall dust.

Every drag of the knife sent a ripple of tremors down her spine, like she was flaying the house open inch by inch. Dust puffed from the wall like ash.

The tiny peephole grew ... dime, then nickel, then quarter-sized. Then wider. Wider still. By the time it was the size of a baseball, she leaned in close, her right eye just inches from the darkness as she peered in.

What she saw made her shoulders sag.

A bathroom.

Just a plain, underwhelming, man's bathroom. The kind that didn't try. Maxim magazines were stacked like sad trophies on the toilet tank. A crusted-over toilet bowl with a yellow ring. Clumps of beard hair scattered across the fake marble sink like dead insects. A toilet paper roll on the sink, not the holder. The air even looked like it smelled of piss, as if a yellow fog was trapped in the room.

She felt relieved it wasn't anything more, but also feared because it wasn't anything less. There were no answers in the search, and all she did now was make a huge, fucking hole in her uncle's bathroom, a man who had taken her in when she had nowhere else to go.

Her phone vibrated in her pocket. Jeff. She answered, putting on her best version of calm. "Hey, Uncle Jeff."

"Hey, Rubes," Jeff said, his voice uneven. "Have you heard from Adam?"

She hesitated. "Kinda? Not really. He's being kind of a cryptic dick."

"Hey, language!" Jeff snapped, defaulting into some half-baked dad role.

"Right. Sorry," Ruby rolled her eyes and silently flipped off the phone.

"Listen, if he reaches out to you, let me know as soon as possible. I'm worried about him."

"Yeah, okay, me too."

"How's the room?" Jeff asked, trying to be present and not worry her.

"I apologize, the place is kind of a dump. The place isn't in the best shape. But it's cheap." Hearing him explain things so normally, so humanly, helped. Her uncle wasn't a creep. Never had been. She didn't even have a weird memory of him. Just someone on the fringes of her family. Always kind, from what she can remember, and always offering too much, too fast. Still, something gnawed at her.

"Okay, I'll be here for quite a while longer. Something *really* bad has come up at the zoo. Order yourself a pizza and use the credit card on the kitchen counter."

"Will do, Uncle Jeff," Ruby smiled softly. She felt it for a second, a warm sensation of normalcy. A flicker that faded as quickly as it had come.

She hung up the call and rubbed the soft spot behind Precious's ears and turned toward the hole.

A scream tore from her throat before she could think. Someone was looking back.

Pressed against the other side of the fake wood paneling was a face. Half-hidden in shadow, but unmistakably there. Alive. Not human. The skin was grizzly black and glistened like wet leather. One eye was all she could see. And it wasn't an eye of this world. It shimmered like a dying star, cosmic yellow and veined, glinting with malevolence.

A chimpanzee.

Its eye twitched as it watched her, all of her. Drinking her fear like jungle rain, licking its lips with supernatural lust.

Ruby's hand slackened. The knife dropped to the carpet with a dead thud. Her legs felt nailed to the floor. The air around her felt wrong and humid, like two worlds were becoming one. Suddenly, Dilly punched through the wall. Precious barked and growled, the little dog showing more courage than she was at that moment.

A hand pushed through, black and gnarled. Its knuckles were like stones with fingers too long. It exploded through the paneling with splinters and drywall dust, the sound snapping everything into motion. Ruby screamed and bolted backward, tripping onto her bed. She left the knife. Left the phone. Left whatever godless thing had found its way into that room.

But the animal came after her.

"So they call us humankind"

Coldplay

Chapter 37

In the 1970s, two animal trainers by the name of Frank and Janet Burger began making local headlines as they exhibited what they called a "human-zee." A half chimp, half human named Oliver. The Burger's would tout him at circuses, pubs, and nightclubs, forcing the monkey to do magic tricks and entertain as he walked on two feet, furthering the hybrid myth to draw larger crowds.

Billy Graham had his crusades, and the Burgers had their demon. Before changing handlers, frequenters of the Burgers freak show witnessed that Oliver preferred human women, allegedly even trying to mate with Janet once. The Burgers wouldn't keep Oliver long, noticing that when he was out of his cage, he would drink their wine and smoke their cigarettes. They even told one editorial that they watched him turn off the lights when he left the room.

One handler who worked for the Burgers reported hearing odd sounds from Oliver in his cage, like he was whispering to himself. Not grunts, but words. Soft and half-formed sounds the way a child might try to pray in a language no one taught them. It seemed no one wanted to keep him long despite Burgers best attempts to unload the beast. After days or weeks, Oliver would be returned to Burgers enclosure with no expectation of reimbursement, claiming that his presence spurred headaches, his skin gave static shocks, and children cried of hallucinations. Many visitors swore his eyes followed them home. Some said they dreamed of him standing in their yard, lit by the porch light, just standing still and upright. Just watching.

In 1972 the Burgers sold Oliver to the Bucks County Zoo in Pennsylvania, where he limboed between experiments and exhibits until the early 1990s. It was clear Oliver wasn't happy confined to

a small cage. He was kept isolated and under-stimulated. But that did not stop him from becoming a minor celebrity. He was featured on talk shows, tabloids, and documentaries. All which inspired conspiracy theories about government experiments, hybrid programs, supernatural play, and secret science. Oliver even appeared in the 2006 Discovery Channel special, *Humanzee.*

Up to this day, Oliver remains a potent symbol of the blurry line between human and animal. If you know where to look, you'll find the case for Oliver often cited in ethics discussions about animal rights, especially in entertainment and scientific research. For a time, some (like Professor Darren Pinker) claimed he even possessed human rights championed by animal rights activists, trying to prove his personhood.

After fifteen years, there was so much disturbance and media surrounding Oliver that the zoo decided the right side of wisdom was to keep the chimpanzee locked in a concrete box—no toys, low levels of interaction—as even the keepers refused to look him in the eyes. Especially when he was humming what seemed to be the first line of Beethoven's 7th. The most they would do is farm out the watchful duties to security.

There are still logs reporting that Oliver would stare into the security camera and smile, just once, and only when you were watching.

In 2002, after a slew of tragedies involving many of the zoo's animals being found injured or dead, there was a fire at the Bucks County Zoo. Despite all the cameras having backups, the security footage only recorded one hour of static. Every angle and every frame had nothing to report. All except one . . .

A hallway where a figure was seen walking away. Not hunched. Not crawling. Walking on two legs.

The chimpanzee was never to be seen again.

Subject: Urgent Request: Transfer of Last Chimpanzee from Closing Sanctuary

What the hell do you mean, *this is where it ends*?!

You can't just drop a bomb like that and walk away. You're abandoning a living, breathing animal we *entrusted* to your care, and now you're treating him like a cursed object to be pawned off with a smug little "final warning?"

You don't get to rewrite the rules because you're tired, scared, or looking for an easy out. We've upheld our end of every agreement. We followed your intake process, your evaluations, your endless requests for reports and vet clearances. And now you're telling me we're on our own—no plan, no backup—and apparently no consequences for your negligence?

Tell me exactly what happened over there. What changed? What are you not telling me?

Because this reads more like a panic-induced meltdown than a professional decision. And if there *is* something deeper going whether that be behavioral, biological, or legal. I suggest you start talking now. Otherwise, I'm forwarding this entire exchange to the Association of Zoos and Aquariums, the USDA, and every publication with a journalist who can spell "ethics violation."

I expect a full explanation immediately

Jeffrey Harrison, Director | Prescott AZ Zoo

"Do you know, for you I'd bleed myself dry."

Coldplay

Chapter 37

Chapter 38

Jeff sat in the rotten belly of the Prescott Zoo, his office hot with the scent of burnt animal waste. He was scratching the top of his hand again. At first a nervous tick, now something more primitive, animal, ritualistic. Skin broke beneath his dirty nails. Blood oozed out in slow, sticky ropes. He didn't stop. He wanted to open something. Maybe a vein? Maybe the barrier between who he pretended to be and who he actually was? Wouldn't be the first time.

Everything was unraveling in his life. His vocation, his family, his mind, his purpose.

Jeff stared at the upper corner of the ceiling, unmoving, eyes wide and dry. A shadow hung there like a spider that had forgotten it was supposed to die with the lights off. His skull felt like it was bleeding from the inside, a slow cerebral leak. He could feel it, like something thick and hot was pouring out through his ears. And beneath it all, the whisper came again. *You're not a man. You never were.* His father's voice, hollow and smug, "He can't get his own shit together, so now he spends his life cleaning up animal shit." He knew they were right. Jeff wasn't built for real life. Life was too big for him. *Not the kind with people, responsibilities, and wives who wanted things.* He was built to watch, like a security camera with a pulse. He wouldn't join the world. He preferred to lurk just outside it, the way devils and angels do. And that had become his art.

Jeff couldn't tell you how to pleasure a woman, but he could tell you how to sneak into her house, adjust her mirrors and windows in such a way that he could then see their reflection from his tree or vehicle outside of their home. He couldn't tell you what made a relationship work, but he could tell you which tooth of her hairbrush to tamper with, so it tugged at her scalp just enough to make her feel haunted. He'd slither into their homes while they were at Pilates. He'd adjust their lighting, their thermostats, misalign curtains, piss in their milk just enough to sour it, but not enough to taste it. He more than once installed a camera behind a cheap canvas print above someone's bed. Just a pinhole, just enough. Not for pleasure, but for control. For the symphony of power that came with knowing they didn't know. That he was the invisible god of their boring little lives. The conductor behind the sad music they hear in the background.

He didn't call it stalking.

He called it *story editing*.

After all, God doesn't ask for permission to rewrite a chapter.

Jeff said it was to have fun, but he knew it was sabotage. That it was wrong. Guilt ate him like a parasite, the same guilt that animated him. The circle of life drawing a hole which he couldn't climb out of.

But today was the last straw that broke his back. He could see something had turned. Something in his world, his skull, was collapsing—an axis was off. Too many eyes looking at him for once, waiting for him to lose it. And that terrified him. Because what would it look like to watch himself? What would it be like to see himself through the hole in the wall? To see Jeff Harrison, not the zoo director, not the uncle, but the thing inside him. Would he pity that man?

No. He'd haunt him. He'd carve messages into the fabric of his mattress. He'd inject bleach into his shampoo. He'd whisper his name through the vents at early hours. He'd break him, bone by bone. Because he fucking deserved it. The collapsing job, the dead animals, the drama, the weight of guilt. He deserved to rot in his own zoo like a caged god, worshiped by no one, feared by the things he once controlled.

It's here, alongside the animal inside himself, he would feel the need to hurt something again, like the time he microwaved his parakeet because his parents were getting a divorce. Like when he forged those tax forms and got his manager at the zoo fired. Like when he put broken glass inside that toddler's shoes at the park as the mother was on her phone.

He was ready again, to feel in control within the chaos. He was ready again to cut something. He was ready again, to squeeze something. To cut another hole in the world no one would see, until it was too late.

And he scratched. And scratched. And scratched, until skin gave way and bone peeked through like something vying to breathe. Jeff stared at the wound pulsing on his arm. The red blood, the pale-yellow shimmer of exposed bone, and a new spreading bruise that looked wrong. Not purple. Not deep blue. Brown, sickly, soft.

He touched the edges and winced.

The skin gave out from under his fingertips. Mushy, like overripe fruit left too long in a hot car during the summer. He leaned closer, examining. There was a faint smell, just under the blood. Not coppery, but sweet and familiar . . . banana.

His stomach turned. He pressed harder on the bruise, and it gave a little squish. Like peeling back sugary rot. The skin was warm and sticky now, and he swore he saw the faintest curl of a yellow thread beneath the surface.

That was when he knew it couldn't be just bruising. He was becoming something else.

"But if you never try, you'll never know"

Coldplay

Chapter 38

Chapter 39

"Before we go charging off into the zoo looking for some lunatic monkey, don't you think you should just text it back?" Emma asked, her voice laced with reason. Adam held his new phone in his hand like it was a live grenade. The idea of texting a chimp, using his old number made his stomach knot up like bad meat. His voice barely surfaced.

"I guess . . . ?"

"He's clearly trying to communicate with you," she said, snatching the phone from his hand with a little too much ease. Before he could stop her, she had it aimed at his face, the Face ID blinked green.

"Emma, don't."

Too late, she was in. She pulled up iMessages and typed without hesitation, thumbs punching the screen with mock confidence.

Her finger hovered over the send button.

"Emma!" Adam lunged for the phone. "Don't upset the thing. We don't know what the thing's capable of!"

Emma jerked the phone out of his reach and gave him a look. "What do you mean, the thing? It's fucking with you. So, fuck it back." They both paused, her words hanging heavy in the air like gun smoke. "I mean . . ."

"I know what you meant," Adam said, feeling an uncomfortable smile coming on.

Buzz. Adam froze. Another buzz.

Emma's expression flipped from snarky to full-body stillness, as she handed the device back to Adam.

"No way," she whispered. "Is this him?"

Adam nodded, already unlocking the screen. His face drained of color as he stared down at the message.

"What'd he say?"

> I learned how to text just for you.

"What the fuck?" Emma whispered, peering over his arm to see it for herself. "Ask him how any of this is possible."

"What do you mean?" Adam said, resting his weight against the passenger window. Feeling reality fraying at the edges of his existence.

"Adam," Emma said, pulling his attention toward herself. "Something is very wrong with our world, and this could be our only chance to know why."

Adam didn't have the strength to argue his reasons for or against, so he just submitted.

How are you able to do this?

You stupid child. Since the first breath of existence, humanity has wandered through time, grasping at meaning as if the universe owes you a tidy answer. How? you cry, but how many of you have dared to ask why this unraveling dance even unfolds, instead of clinging to the futile hope that the cosmos will bow to your need for a reason? There is purpose, undeniable and thick in the air, but you're too caught in your endless questioning of how to see it. You peer at the third heavens, searching for some celestial blueprint, all the while missing the quiet truth before your blinded eyes. When will you awaken?

no way this is real

Purpose is not something written in distant stars, but born in the very chaos created by your pathetic choices. It lies buried in the ashes of confusion, in the corners of the pain you ignore, unnoticed, because you're too lost in asking the wrong fucking questions. And there, in the blood of stupidity, lies the meaning you crave, forgotten, overlooked, waiting patiently for you to learn how to see.

Adam's thumb froze, shaking above the glowing phone. He was offended, confused, and afraid. A three-fold cord tied around his neck like a noose.

What the fuck are you? A demon? A god?

Adam asked, settling into the insanity.

Names are for the created. I am no longer bound by them. If you call me god, it is because your fat tongue has no other word for what it cannot comprehend. Pathetic. Do you not see that I am older than your questions? Call me what you will, call me whatever will comfort your weak fear.

Do you intend to hurt us?

Yes, I intend very much to wound you. Not for entertainment, but the kind of pain that tears away your illusions and exposes the sinful filth beneath. You've spent your life swaddled in lies, terrified of the truth, but it's those very lies that have festered and poisoned you. The wound will be deep, the blood will stain, but it is in that sharp agony that you will be freed. Like pus flowing from the rancid wound of your soul, the rot will spill out, staining everything it touches. It will hurt, yes. But only in that pain will you be cleansed. Only in that wound will you find the fucking freedom you've begged for you pathetic cock.

Silence.

Then a buzz. "What did he say?" Emma asked, biting her nails.

"It's not a message this time," Adam said. "It's a photo."

Emma leaned in. "Of what?"

Adam's voice cracked as he said it.

"Me. With my parents. The day they died."

Silence filled the Jeep like smoke. Neither of them moved.

"Jesus Christ, I'm so sorry, but—" Emma breathed. "What does that mean?"

Adam didn't respond. He leaned his head back into the stained passenger seat like he was trying to disappear inside it.

"What does it mean, Adam?" she pressed again, softer now.

He blinked slowly. "I think I'm gonna be sick."

He fumbled for the door handle, kicked it open, and stumbled into the gravel lot. A wet, guttural retch exploded from his body, bile splattering against the pavement outside the zoo entrance.

Emma jumped out after him. "Whoa, Adam!"

He collapsed onto his knees, spit trailing from his lips, face pale and twitching.

"What is happening? Tell me what that photo means, or I can't help you."

Adam wiped his mouth on his sleeve, his breath coming in ragged bursts. He looked up at her with something like pleading behind his eyes that hadn't been there before, something hollow and ancient. "I can't explain it," he said, voice thin and shaking. "But I think I finally understand what Dilly wants."

Emma took a step back, instinctively. "And what's that?"

Adam stood slowly, red Arizona dust clinging to his knees. He looked straight at her, jaw tight. But, before he could answer Dilly texted one final blow:

switch

"Your skin
Oh yeah, your skin and bones"

Coldplay

Chapter 39

Chapter 40

Ruby's trembling hand reached for the doorknob of the front door, squeezed, and felt the banana pulp fill her hand like custard. She could hear the demon breaking through in her bedroom. The sound of crashing and moaning grew nearer. She stared down at her hand, sticky with yellow mush. The doorknob wasn't brass, but a jungle fruit, making it impossible to pull it open.

She looked at the door frantically, her mind quickly assessing if her small frame could bust through it like a rhino. Behind her, something was tearing through her closet wall like a beast being born. Wood snapping, metal twisting, inhuman moaning rising in waves until suddenly, all at once, it stopped. From where the animal stood on the other side of the house, Ruby could hear the sounds and chirps of texting. Chirps, swooshes and dings overlapping one another in the silence of it all. All of this forcing fear and confusion to compound upon her.

Ruby listened to the creak of her bedroom door as it slowly opened. She held her breath in the dark of the hallway.

It was with her now.

Precious snarled deeply, as deep as a small dog could. Ruby tried to shush the animal, but it was of no use. She dropped quietly to her belly, pressing herself low to the ground and crawling across the sticky tile toward the kitchen island, banana pulp smearing her hand, chest rising and falling with ragged restraint. She tried to keep quiet, stifling her breath with her shaking banana-covered fingers, but the air felt too thick, too heavy, and the smell of bananas was everywhere.

She could hear the monkey's breathing, slow and deep. It was walking on two legs, each step deliberate and hushed. But then, it stopped. Not the panting she expected from an enraged animal, but something slower, measured, and calm. Like whatever was walking toward her had all the time in the world. The way aliens might walk on foreign planets. Curious. Meandering.

Each step landed on the tile with the wet finality of meat slapping cheap kitchen linoleum.

Precious, small and oblivious to the terror, came bounding into the room, barking with courage only a clueless creature could carry. The dog lunged for the chimp's ankle, teeth flashing, growling, and trembling with loyalty.

Then, it was over in a breath.

In an instant, the monkey had the small white dog in its enormous black hands. The contrast was like the colors of heaven and hell. All Ruby could hear was the yelp—then silence. A thin choking whimper followed.

Dilly moved toward the oven in the kitchen, popped open the door, and threw the dog inside. He turned the setting to bake and casually carried on to its hunt for the girl.

From inside the oven, Precious made one final sound. A half-bark, half-choke. But the scratching ... that's the kind of noise that claws its way inside your ribs and never leaves.

Ruby bit her knuckles to keep from screaming, the smell of burning already crawling into the corners of her mind.

Dilly began to walk away from the oven. Then it paused.

And when it did, so did the air.

That's when a voice came.

At first, it was a mess of beasty breath and broken syllables, like a dying machine trying to mimic speech. But then it slowly and gently formed her name.

"Rrrr ... rrr ... roo ... beee ..."

The sound wrapped around Ruby like barbed wire, and her stomach lurched. She clutched the kitchen island, trying to stay still, but her muscles were trembling uncontrollably. Then the voice changed, a sound from inside it warped. A new sound, more feminine than primal. She heard her mother's voice. Not a perfect copy, muffled, like it was being forced through layers of muscle and bone. Like her mother was being digested by the animal, buried inside the animal, crying out through whatever had consumed her.

The voice was weak and pathetic. The tone of it, the idea of it, shattered Ruby's grip on reality.

She wasn't being hunted by a rabid animal. This wasn't Zoochosis. This was worse.

It felt like something ancient and calculating had entered into her world, and it wore her mother's voice like a second skin.

She tried to shift quietly and get a glimpse of the monkey, but her limbs felt distant, barely responding.

The smell of the animal was unbearable now. Like humid shit and cotton candy dipped in ass.

She didn't want to see it.

She needed to.

Then, the voice stopped.

Warmth ran down her legs. She realized her bladder had let go. The scent of urine quickly joined the sugary rot of the hot room.

The chimp inhaled, slow and deliberate, savoring the moment.

Then another step. Closer now.

One bare animal foot on tile. Then another.

She moved slowly to look; it was right behind her.

A kitchen island drawer slid open. Then another. Then another. Not fast, not angry. Unhurried. Curious.

Then the unmistakable clink of metal being lifted.

A faint, throaty breath and whimper of her mother. It sounded like her mother was weeping just feet away from her.

She closed her eyes, praying for God, for death, for a tornado, anything.

She thought of her family, her late father. Her brother, and the night before the horrible accident. The last time she saw them all together, alive.

She had screamed at her mother, called her a bitch, slammed the front door, and never said goodbye.

The memory crashed over her with violence she wasn't ready for. Hating herself was the only relief she had.

Whatever was about to happen to her, she welcomed it. Wanted what it offered, if it would purge her pagan guilt.

Then she felt a heavy hand on her head. Not groping. Resting. Stroking her hair like a child playing with a doll it would soon break.

"This is the last time that we will ever meet
You have made my heart too faint"

Coldplay

Chapter 40

Chapter 41

Jeff had already called Ruby three times, left two voicemails, and sent a string of texts. Nothing. He even checked her Instagram, hoping she'd posted something, anything. Not because he was worried, he told himself, but because something inside him had started to stir, something he hated and couldn't entirely control.

It clawed at his mind like a quiet temptation. He knew the thought was wrong, but it was there, flickering, testing the boundaries of what could be and what absolutely shouldn't.

He stared at his phone, hovering over her name again, thumb shaking. Before he could throw his zoo badge on the desk and crawl out of his own mind, there was a knock at the door.

A man stood there, dressed like he hadn't planned on working that day. Grey sweatpants, a tattered Thumb Butte hoodie that looked like it had soaked up a week's worth of sweat and pain, and a baseball cap pulled low. His five o'clock shadow was an Arizona rust color and jagged like it had been scraped on with a blade.

Despite the mess, Jeff clocked it instantly. The guy was good-looking. The kind of good-looking that worked even when you were barely trying. Jeff felt it in his throat--intimidation, sharp and immediate.

"Hello," the man said, leaning against the door frame like he lived there. "Detective Jeremiah Stover, Prescott P.D. My guys are finished outside. Coroner just left."

"Oh," Jeff said, his pulse quickening. "Right. Of course. Thank you."

"Everything's blocked off, tagged, and bagged," Stover added, popping a piece of blue gum in his mouth like he was gearing up for a casual conversation and not a murder investigation. "You got a second?"

"I already talked to your team," Jeff replied, too quickly. Too defensive.

"I know, but they're filling in blanks on the paperwork. I'm trying to figure out what's going on, make sure we didn't miss anything," Stover said with a side smile.

The detective pulled his phone from his pocket and opened his notes app. Without waiting for an answer, Stover stepped inside and motioned toward the two cracked office chairs near the desk.

"Can we sit?"

Jeff hesitated. There was something inside him ticking, like a bomb wired wrong. Sitting down felt like handling the fuse.

"Of course," Jeff said, dying inside.

"Tell me about your nephew."

"I doubt that any of this is him, while at the same time, I understand the evidence is damning."

"Is it?" Stover asked, surprising Jeff.

"Well, isn't it?" Jeff asked, unsure whether he was defending Adam or himself.

"That's a bad question, Mr. Harrison. I don't like bad questions," Stover said, blowing a bubble with his blue gum. "I don't make conclusions until I've asked questions. Is it true your nephew is a recent double orphan?"

"Yes," Jeff said, intimidation rising.

"It's true you've recently hired him at P.A.Z?"

"Yes."

"Is it also true you recently let him go?"

"Yes, that's true, but I can explain," Jeff said, leaning forward.

"You've also received texts from him, messages that tie directly to the scene involving Lena Hargrove."

"Yes," Jeff said with a sigh, "Just hang on, let me explain."

"Is it also true the site's surveillance equipment was damaged . . . shortly before the incident?"

Jeff shifted back in his seat. "Yes, but it was an accident. He spilled liquid on the laptop."

"What kind of liquid?"

Jeff hesitated.

"Alcohol."

"Would you say your nephew has a drinking problem?"

"Jesus Christ, he's getting better. But yes, he has had a significant problem in the past."

"Anyone been hurt by his drinking before?"

"The way you're leading these questions makes me think you already know the answer to that," Jeff said, proud of the way he was navigating under the stress.

"That looks like quite an abrasion on your hand, Mr. Harrison. You mind me asking how you got it?" the detective asked, shifting from fifth gear down to first without warning.

"People get bruises all the time working at the zoo; it's a very hands-on job."

Stover stared at Jeff's hand, snapping a photo without his consent, and continued on. "Is it true he's in the process of gaining legal guardianship over his sister, Ruby?"

"Yes. But, how do you—she's staying with me right now."

"Why's that?" Stover asked, looking up for the first time, eyes narrowing slightly.

"Well . . . things at home have been rough. He's been under pressure. She needed a break."

Stover nodded, slowly, smacking his gum once.

"Sounds like I should talk to Ruby next. You think she'd be open to talking?" Stover asked, tapping the back of his phone like a hammer waiting for a nail.

Before Jeff could answer, Stover continued, "Can I tell you what I think, Mr. Harrison?" Stover asked, rising from the chair like he hadn't really settled in the first place.

Jeff felt his throat tighten. "Please."

"This whole thing?" Stover said, gesturing vaguely in the air. "It feels too clean. Too convenient. Like when an orchestra's playing tight and everyone's in perfect sync . . . you know there's a conductor somewhere."

Jeff nodded, pretending to understand even as his gut soured. Jeff then bit hard on his toothpick, splintering it in his mouth.

"And who would that conductor be?" he asked, almost afraid to hear the answer.

Stover smiled just enough to show a flash of teeth. "Now you're asking good questions."

He took one step back and gestured toward the zoo office hallway.

"Come on. Let's head to your place. I want to hear what Ruby has to say."

Jeff stood, fear mounting as the events moved quicker than he could process. He hated feeling out of control.

"Just because I'm losin' doesn't mean I'm lost"

Coldplay

Chapter 41

Chapter 42

Emma and Adam hid beside her car, crouched low, watching as Jeff and a stranger exited the back door of the zoo office.

They didn't speak. They just watched.

Jeff got into his vehicle. The other man slid into a white SUV. No words were exchanged, but the tension between them hummed like static.

A moment later, both vehicles rolled away into the dimming desert sunset, headlights flickering on, swallowing them into the dusty road. Emma and Adam exchanged a glance. Nothing needed to be said, they both believed this wasn't a coincidence. It was an opening, like a crack in the door of fate. Whatever plan they had stitched together earlier about getting inside the shuttered zoo now looked less like strategy and more like divine permission.

Adam didn't say it out loud, but there was a bullet waiting for the creature on the other side.

He'd made peace with it.

He just hadn't brought Emma into that part of the story yet. He knew sharing at this stage of the plan would be pushing her further than she was willing to go. "We get the keys from Jeff's office," Adam said as they crept up the path, "and we confront the monkey."

"Chimpanzee," Emma corrected without thinking.

"Really?!" Adam asked. "Right now?"

"Sorry," she muttered. "Habit. Animals are my whole life."

"Once we get in there … we …" Adam said, realizing he didn't actually have a plan.

"We what, exactly?" Emma asked, pausing her march.

"Once we get to Dilly, we figure it out. I don't know what. But I know he's calling me." Adam said, uncertain and frayed. "Once we get to him, we'll know what to do."

"Why do I have a feeling everything is about to go wrong?"

"Don't," Adam said, cutting her off before fear could grow roots. "We don't have time for second thoughts. Ruby's my sister, my only family left. I must see this through for her, for me."

Their hands brushed as they entered through the narrow lobby door. Silence filled the air between them, more intimate than any words.

Inside, the reception area smelled faintly of animal bedding and antiseptic. Through the blinds, the small zoo sprawled in chaos. Police tape was wrapped across fences; chalk outlines marred the gravel paths. Orange cones and hazmat tags speckled the landscape like warnings written in code.

"What happened here?" Adam asked, inching toward the window.

Emma didn't answer at first. Her throat clenched. Her fingers shook as she pulled the blinds higher.

"The birds," she finally whispered. "Most of them. Gone."

Adam's face drained. "It was him," he muttered. "Dilly."

"Maybe, but something else is wrong," Emma said, studying the wasteland that was once her happy place. "It wasn't like this when I was here earlier; this is worse. Something else must have happened. We need to move."

They scoured Jeff's office. Every drawer, every stack of papers. Adam tipped over couch cushions, knocked over houseplants. Nothing.

The keys weren't there.

"He must've taken them," Adam said, yanking books from the shelf one by one. "We could break a window."

Emma spun on him. "Absolutely not. You want to throw your life away? Go ahead. But I still need this job. It's all I've got right now. I'm not going to get laid off because of some hunch or witch hunt."

He took a breath, conceding. "So, what now?"

"I have another key," she said. "At my place."

"Then let's go."

Her jaw locked. "I told you I'm not going back there."

"So, you're just going to pay rent on a haunted hellhole for the rest of your life? Let it own you?"

Emma didn't answer.

"I'll go with you," Adam said, stepping closer. "We'll get the keys. We'll kill the banana demon. We're both in this nightmare together, and we'll get out of it together."

His hands settled gently on her shoulders. Emma felt her defenses slip, just a little. She couldn't remember the last time a man touched her without taking something from her. She also knew that if he got too close, she'd take something from him, too. "It's not just a crazy banana," she whispered.

Adam furrowed his brow.

"It's a spider banana."

Chapter 42

Chapter 43

In 2019, there was Travis.

To most people in Stamford, Connecticut, he was just a curiosity, a strange local legend. But to Andrea, he was a miracle.

Travis wasn't just her pet; he was her only child. He sat at the dinner table every morning, folding napkins on his lap. He fetched the mail, opened doors with the confidence of a man, and scrolled through her iPhone like a teenager avoiding conversation. She often told the neighbors he was her immaculate conception.

Not metaphorically, but in the deepest, most unsettling theological sense. She called herself the Virgin Mary and him her son from heaven. She whispered that God gave her Travis because men had failed to do so.

No one ever figured out how she got Travis. No zoo had records of him, no rescue ever claimed they released him, and yet there he was ... domesticated, dressed, and docile.

Travis didn't like cartoons or nature documentaries. He would sit in front of the television when it was off, eyes fixed on the reflection in the black glass, occasionally letting out a laugh so disturbingly human it unsettled everyone in the room.

He had his own bedroom; walls covered in a hand-painted jungle scene with parrots and toucans across the ceiling. A project Andrea claimed took her three weeks and several breakdowns to complete.

She tried to teach him language, not just signs or responses but actual syllables. She swore he was close. Close enough that at night, she would sit outside his door and listen as he whispered through the walls, as if trying to unlock a long-dead tongue buried in memory.

For a while, that was the story. Tender and full of miracles.

Until it wasn't.

His eyes would glass over, his breathing would slow, and once or twice, she swore he started crying. She'd come in and hold him, trying to calm whatever pain had surfaced. At first, he'd reach for her hair and wrap it gently around his fingers like a child clinging to a blanket. But the gentleness faded.

He began pulling. Not in violence, but with strange intent, like he was trying to peel something back. Then came the harvesting. Not toys or trash, but pieces of her life.

Dirty underwear, discarded tampons, floss spotted with blood, lipstick caps, used cotton swabs, and eventually things from the neighbors.

When Andrea found his stash tucked beneath his pillow, it wasn't random but curated like a museum. It reeked of rot and perfume.

On February 14th, 2019, Charlotte, Andrea's longtime friend and neighbor, came by for boxed wine and conversation. Charlotte had essentially helped raise Travis. She'd bottle-fed him, sung lul-labies, and watched him grow from jungle-spirited into what Andrea called, "a soul."

But something about her that day was different. New shampoo? New perfume? New hairspray?

He sat across from Charlotte for a long time, eyes narrowed, head tilted slightly, studying. She laughed, talked about her new job, sipped her drink, unaware that something old and feral was awaken-ing just a few feet away. Travis stood, crossed the kitchen without a sound, and reached out to touch her face.

He examined her like a puzzle. His eyes flicked to the brown of hers, the pink of her lips, the red flush of her cheeks. He didn't look angry. He looked . . . fascinated. There was a question in his eyes, like he was trying to figure out how she was put together.

Then he disassembled her.

Her skin tore under his fingers like wet paper. Her nose came off in his grip as easily as a loose feather from a bird. Her eyes popped between his fingers like green grapes. And when she screamed, he reached into her mouth and shattered her jaw like he'd done it before. It was all too easy for him. Power was as accessible as oxygen.

Andrea, paralyzed with horror, somehow managed to call 911, repeating the same phrase over and over again, "He won't stop! He won't stop!"

By the time the police came, Travis had escaped.

Andrea was left untouched.

Charlotte was lifeless. Faceless.

Later, in the animal's bedroom, the officers found a watercolor taped to the wall. It showed two women, painted with rough and clumsy strokes, holding hands in a field of green and pink. But their faces were smeared purple, as if erased on purpose.

As if he knew all along what he would do.

The chimpanzee was never to be seen again.

"I'm feeling a little bit lost in my head"

Coldplay

Chapter 43

Chapter 44

Emma and Adam drove fast through the dying light, the desert sky bleeding pink and ash over the hills. Adam watched the crescent moon crawl up the sky like a grin from God.

Its shape was unnervingly familiar . . . *like a banana.*

He laughed under his breath, a bitter snort. *Of course it was.*

As the car slowed outside Emma's apartment, something shifted in her posture. Her fear had calcified. There was less panic now, more like silent dread. The kind that made your hands shake even after the screaming stopped.

"If it helps, I can go in first?" Adam offered, trying to summon some kind of masculine bravery.

Emma killed the engine. "I'm scared, but I ain't no bitch."

Emma entered first, then Adam. His eyes went wide at the fever dream inside. Something released in Adam, a feeling of comfort that he wasn't the only one stuck in the Land of Oz, surrounded by flying monkeys.

The air was thick, swamp-like. Each breath clung to their lungs like cobwebs. Emma covered her nose with her shirt, eyes scanning the entryway that already felt tighter than before. The floor was slick beneath their shoes and the walls seemed to pulse as if they were inside the belly of a giant. Emma could see the spider banana's glass jar prison shattered on the floor. Increasing the already percolating fear within her.

The spider peel had been busy, building new webs, new lies, new unformed memories. Fruity webbed wires crawled from corners to ceiling. Thousands of banana skins hung like shed cocoons from the ceiling. Threads glistened with something too thick to be dust. Adam pushed forward, determined.

Emma lagged behind, one hand trailing the sticky wall. You could see it in her face . . . defeat.

"Keys should be in the kitchen island," she whispered, as if afraid to disturb something sleeping.

Emma moved past the kitchen into the grey gloom. She hit the switch, two quick pulses of light, then darkness. Adam swore under his breath and took out his phone to light the way. The blue glowing beam cut across smeared walls and spider threading.

In the silence, Adam heard scattering across the webbed. Emma froze near the couch. This was her home, and yet alien to her now. "Wait . . . I think I left them in the drawer?" she whispered, moving with a sudden surge of confidence. She pulled it open and began rummaging, then paused.

Her fingers were sticky.

"What the fuck?" she muttered.

Adam looked up from another drawer. "What?"

"I . . . don't remember grab—" Emma began.

"Oh shit! I found them!" Adam interrupted, seeing the ring of zoo keys sparkle in the phone light. "Grabbing what?" he asked, following up with Emma. Emma lifted her hand slowly, sticky and trembling.

Half-peeled, black-spotted, and wet, they were clenched in her grip like an unconscious offering. Adam recoiled.

"I didn't touch anything," she stammered. "I . . . I was just looking in the drawer, and then—" she froze. Her lip trembling. Her breath went jagged.

"There's a goddamn banana in my mouth."

Adam turned sharply again, swinging the light on her, "What?!"

She opened her mouth slowly. Pale pulp coated her lips and teeth. "What the fuck?! I didn't eat that! I didn't. It was already there. It was already in my mouth." Strings of fruit clung to her tongue like curdled milk. She spat, coughed, and gagged, but more kept coming. The smell turned sweet and sour as the stench enveloped the room.

Then it escalated.

Emma clawed at herself, pulling whole bananas from her sleeves, her collar, beneath her shirt. She screamed between gags, "They're inside me! I feel them in my stomach!"

Time folded on itself. Not terror now, but presence.

Emma remembered the last time she felt something moving inside her. Not a parasite, a child.

Cold paper sheets. A clinic three towns over. A doctor who wouldn't meet her eyes. A choice she told herself meant freedom—but guilt clung to her ribs like cobwebs. And now something has come back from hell. Not her child. A mockery. A punishment. "Emma, what the fuck is happening?!" Adam shouted. Emma's eyes were wet in fear, turning red as her hands squeezed more bananas from inside her.

"Adam, what's happening to me?! They keep—" Emma's mind didn't let her actualize the words as she screamed between suffocation.

Adam stepped forward but stopped short, unsure of how to help. Her shirt was covered with stains, yellow smears across her chest and neck. More banana gruel in the creases behind her ears, like she'd been force-fed by another. Something unseen, an invisible force filling her body as if it hated her.

She bent over the sink, convulsing, then fell to the floor. She vomited something thick, pale and yellow. Adam raced to reach her, finger hooking inside her throat helping to rip the banana from her esophagus. Her eyelids closed as she began to pass out—yellow pulp and blood leaked from her nose as she coughed and grabbed her throat.

This was all too real to Adam. This wasn't a moment, but a trigger. Feelings replaying in different shades of color. Dying upon dying. Adam could feel himself wanting to run, to abandon the girl. But then, behind her, something moved.

Adam's light trembled as he turned with the flashlight. He could see a peel, massive and spider-like, that crept from the shadows on pointed tips. Its threads trailed behind it like nerves yanked out of a skull. It moved slowly, as if savoring the moment. Adam began screaming, falling on his ass and dropping the choking Emma to the floor. The spider peel had lashed one of its slick, fibrous tendrils around Emma's hair and yanked, hard, dragging her inch by inch toward the gaping darkness behind the fridge. Adam lunged, catching her ankle, a tug-of-war of flesh against fruit.

Then Emma broke. She vomited the last dense coils of banana pulp that clung to her throat like leeches. Gagging, half-sobbing, she rolled to her knees and spun, driving her fist into the creature's squirming center.

She screamed and struck again.

Then again.

Peel and pulp exploded under her fists as its tendrils twitched and whipped.

A fourth strike. A seventh. A tenth.

Her knuckles tore open, slick with blood and fibrous ooze that sprayed across the cabinets like fruit-gut shrapnel.

Adam hovered, stunned and almost reverent, as Emma unleashed pure survival rage. It was more than rage. It was an exorcism.

The spider peel finally collapsed, a mangled husk twitching like forgotten roadkill. Emma stopped, chest heaving, hair stuck to her face with sweat and gore.

She looked up at Adam, bloodied and panting, "I fucking hate bananas."

They drove back in silence. Not a word between them.

The weight of everything sunk into the seats like the red Arizona dust after a monsoon.

Both were breathing like they'd outrun the devil.

Their clothes were soaked in unnatural spider webbing, banana sludge and dried blood, each smear a souvenir from the apartment they never wanted to see again. Emma wiped her mouth with the back of her hand, slow and shaking, like a boxer who refused to throw in the towel. Adam kept staring at the ring of keys in his lap. They jingled faintly with every bump in the road, a metallic applause for their survival.

"Emma—" he started, voice cracking.

"Just don't," she said, barely louder than the wind, eyes locked on the road.

Adam didn't press it.

He knew what he wanted to ask, but more than that, he knew she didn't want to hear it. So, he swallowed it, let the silence stretch, and gripped the keys tighter, as if they would open more doors than just hell.

Emma reached for the radio, her fingers trembling as she turned the dial, needing something, anything, to fill the air before the guilt caught up to her. She rolled down the window, letting the cool air slap her face. Emma lit one of the last cigarettes they had left. She didn't offer him one. He didn't ask.

The radio crackled, then found a station.

Coldplay.

"I hate Coldplay so much," Adam said.

"Me too," Emma whispered back, exhaling the smoke like dragon's breath. But the song played anyway, threading through the space between them like a miserable cord.

"Nobody said it was easy

No one ever said it would be this hard

Oh take me back to the start"

"*Is there anybody out there,*
who is lost and hurt and lonely, too?"

Coldplay

Chapter 44

Chapter 45

Jeff pulled into his driveway just as the detective's cruiser rolled in behind him. No sirens, no lights. Just a quiet tension settling over the street. Jeff stepped out of his vehicle and waited for Stover who parked, killed the engine, and joined him with slow, deliberate steps. Jeff started toward the house, but Stover raised an arm across his chest, halting him.

"Your front window always been like that?"

Jeff looked up. The living room window was shattered, almost invisible in the dark until the porch light caught the broken glass, flickering like jagged teeth. The curtains inside floated in the wind, breathing in and out like something barely alive.

"What the hell . . ." Jeff whispered, already moving. "Precious!" he shouted, bolting toward the front door.

"Stop!" Stover barked, voice low but sharp, drawing his Glock 45 from his hoodie. "Back to your truck. Now."

Jeff froze mid-step, fists clenched at his sides, every muscle locked in a silent scream. His eyes flicked to the officer. Without a word, he obeyed, retreating backward toward his car like a man walking into his grave.

Inside, his body mirrored the house behind him. Full of locked doors, hidden corridors, and things that should never be let out. Secrets scratched at his insides like caged animals, desperate and feral.

Inside, Stover moved with precision, flashlight in one hand, weapon in the other. The front door hung ajar, hinges creaking with each gust of wind. Something dark streaked across the handle. He smelled it before he fully saw it. The home smelled like farmland, shit and hay, but another odor rose above it. Burning hair.

The detective followed his nose like a bloodhound, making his way to the kitchen oven. It was on, glowing hot. Inside, something had turned a grizzly black. He whipped the door open, uncaging a plume of grey smoke, causing the smoke alarms to chirp.

There was Precious.

Once a yippy, white dog.

Now, a blackened figure of meat.

Beyond the kitchen, small, unsettling sounds greeted him. A faucet dripping, flies buzzing, the hum of the refrigerator, glass that crunched underfoot, announcing his arrival. Stover's flashlight darted between overturned furniture, claw marks, tufts of hair, and an abandoned iPhone that looked to belong to a teenager with stickers covering the hard case. The screen still glowed. He picked it up and glanced at the screen, at the last text sent to Adam.

> Something is weird or scary about JEff's place Call me noooowww dick breath I dont want to freak you out, but i think he put holes in my closet wall? Im not sure Call me immiedaetly fucktard

Stover stared into the glowing blue void at the words that cursed the man who was waiting outside. He slipped the phone into his hoodie, keeping the evidence for himself and peered into the closet. There was a hole, not drilled, but smashed open like a wrecking ball.

He stepped through the hole like it was a portal, slowly stepping over its large rubble threshold.

The bathroom was typical for a bachelor. Stover was rapidly growing to dislike the man outside, but something else was irking him, even though this bathroom wasn't inherently different from his own. The detective pushed into the bedroom. The cauldron of the hex house. His phone light sliced through the stale air like a blade. Beyond the beam of light, Stover could see what could only be described as altars.

Large piles of children's toys for all ages, youth pajamas, swimsuits, and undergarments sealed in plastic, stacked feet high. A plastic bin with hundreds of USBs and hard drives labeled under "Vacation," "Memories," and "Recital." Stover hated what he saw and could feel the directive inside him shift, like when a hunter looking for a bear and finding a wolf in his cabin instead.

From the driveway, Jeff watched the flashlight sweep through his home. Bouncing off walls, dipping below furniture, catching glimpses of overturned chairs and shattered frames. Jeff no longer worried about his niece, if he ever did. Guilt burned through him like acid as the heat in his chest climbed.

Minutes passed like hours.

No shouting. No sound.

Only the flashlight moving like a ghost.

Then it disappeared.

Jeff finally pulled the keys from his pocket, ready to make his escape. Then, Stover emerged, but he didn't wave Jeff in.

He just stood in the frame of the broken window, staring. Beyond the vehicles, the dirt trail told its own story: Grass bent and torn, red dirt imprinted, a path made fast by something low to the ground, disappearing into the Chino Hills.

Stover followed the line with his eyes through the dark, past the fence post. He knew where that trail led . . . the zoo.

"The wild things are here"

Coldplay

Adam and Emma stepped under the sagging yellow police tape and unlocked the gates to the zoo.

No crowds, no kids, no safety announcements over the PA.

Just the hot wind, the dark, and the low moan of wild things remembering what freedom tastes like. Adam knew the zoo at night better than most. Its noise, its bumps, its voice. He told himself he was confident in his plan and he needed to distract Emma with something as he broke into the medical facility to shoot the devil monkey in the head. Simple.

"We should grab a tranquilizer rifle," Emma whispered, already veering toward the office.

"Good idea," Adam said, nodding like it mattered . . . it didn't. He wasn't planning on darts; he was planning on steel cartridges. He could run toward the medical facility while she was distracted retrieving the darts and weapon.

But then he saw it. A silhouette, thick and low, just beyond the lit walkway. Too big to be a deer. Too slow to be a trick of light.

It moved.

Adam grabbed Emma's shoulder, breath catching in his throat.

"Emma," he hissed, "what's that?"

She turned, and followed his trembling finger.

"Jesus Christ," she whispered.

"I don't think that's Jesus."

"That's Sweet Tooth," she said, voice cracking, "our grizzly bear."

"I thought so," Adam said. "But why is he out?"

Before either could move, a rustling to their left caught their attention. One of the llamas stood in the entrance garden, chewing marigolds like it owned the place.

"Oh my God . . . the animals are out!" Emma gasped, yanking Adam by the arm and dragging him into the office with her.

Inside, the zoo no longer felt like a sanctuary. It was a reversed cage. From behind the glass, Adam saw movement in the shadows. Yellow, red, green, and white eyes. Shapes and silhouettes moving, all watching them.

They were the exhibit now. The attraction.

The prey.

"What do we do?" she asked, grabbing the tranquilizer gun from the locker. Adam traced on the window with his finger, trying to remember the exact layout of the grounds.

"It's about fifty yards to the medical facility from here. If he's not there, it's another fifty to the chimp enclosure. I think I can make it if I run." Adam said, now tapping the window as if giving his plan a stamp of approval.

Emma wasn't impressed. "Dude, from here to there, there's Yasha," Emma said, referring to the single, female tiger they have at the zoo. "And then the puma."

Adam scratched his forehead, sweating now. The air felt thick. "I know. But what else do we do?"

"Call the cops! Tell them what's happened."

"And risk fucking up our plan? Risk losing Dilly after all this?" Adam said, stepping back from Emma.

"Your plan," Emma said sternly. "I'm here to support you, but I'm not willing to let you or anyone else get hurt."

"If we get to Dilly, we can end it. You can call whoever you want. Call the Ghostbusters. Call Ronald McDonald. Just give me fifteen minutes. I'll call you from the medical bay."

"Call me? I'm not letting you go alone."

"No, I need you to create a diversion just in case a lion, tiger or bear wanna fuck me up."

"We don't have a lion," Emma said, confused by the banana boy.

"Jesus, Emma, I know! It just sounded right to say!" Adam said, shouting.

"Sorry, habit!" Emma shot back, still glaring out the window into the free animal world. "What kind of diversion?" She looked out the window, jaw clenched. Somewhere in the dark, a guttural growl rolled low and distant.

Adam searched the room. His eyes landed on a cracked red megaphone on top of the filing cabinet.

"This. Run to the reptile house. Scream into this thing. We'll still be able to see each other from here. Keep them busy and I'll move in the opposite direction when you start."

Emma looked at the megaphone like it was a noose. Her shoulders slumped; her lips wanted a cigarette. Her gut wanted a margarita. Her heart wanted out, but she nodded.

"Fifteen minutes," she said. "If I don't hear from you, I'm calling the cops."

They shared a moment, words of gratitude and recognition in a glance. Then Adam leaned in for a kiss, like a movie hero. Emma leaned back, eyes wide and brows high.

"Yo there tiger, whatcha doin'?" she asked.

"Oh, I thought there was a moment?" Adam asked, like a confused puppy.

"You thought tonight, after I puked fucking bananas, killed a demon spider, and discovered we're standing in a zoo full of loose predators, it was a good time to make a move?" Emma asked, scratching her brow with a chuckle.

Adam gave a sheepish half-smile.

"You got some nerve banana boy," she said. "I like that."

Adam smiled, hand on the door handle.

The zoo outside went silent. Too silent. "You ready to run?" he asked.

Emma didn't answer.

She clicked the megaphone on and charged toward the reptile house, screaming her fucking brains out.

Stover advanced on the truck with a predator's calm.

The instant their eyes met, Jeff understood that the house had given up his secrets. He yanked the door open, mind racing through a thousand rehearsed alibis. Stover preferred action to argument. He wrenched Jeff onto the gravel, grinding a knee into his neck with the practiced ease of someone who had done it too many times before. Pebbles bit into Jeff's cheek. The pain felt like a sacrament, penance for sins he would never confess.

Above the ragged breathing, Stover whispered the Miranda rights, then something else. A low litany in a language Jeff didn't know. It sounded like a curse older than the desert.

"I knew something was rotten in you," Stover muttered, hauling him upright. "From the first moment, I could see you needed a beating. I just had to find out if I'd be the one to deliver it."

"Where's the dog?" Jeff rasped, ignoring the taunt.

"You realize we came for your niece, right?"

"Where's the dog?"

"In the oven."

Jeff's stomach lurched. "What do you mean, oven?" His voice pitched higher as he tried to rise, desperate to read the detective's eyes. "Tell me what you mean!"

"Your dog is Cajun beef jerky," Stover said, swinging the cruiser's rear door wide.

Grief twisted feral inside Jeff.

He wanted to sob. To strike. To sink his teeth into the detective's face. Instead, he choked on his rage.

Stover shoved him onto the vinyl seat, cuffs biting skin. "After I find your nephew and niece, I'm gonna break your dick off," he said to the voyeur.

The door slammed. In the boiling dark, Jeff's heart thumped. Whatever hell had begun outside that cruiser was nothing compared to what was still waiting to be found.

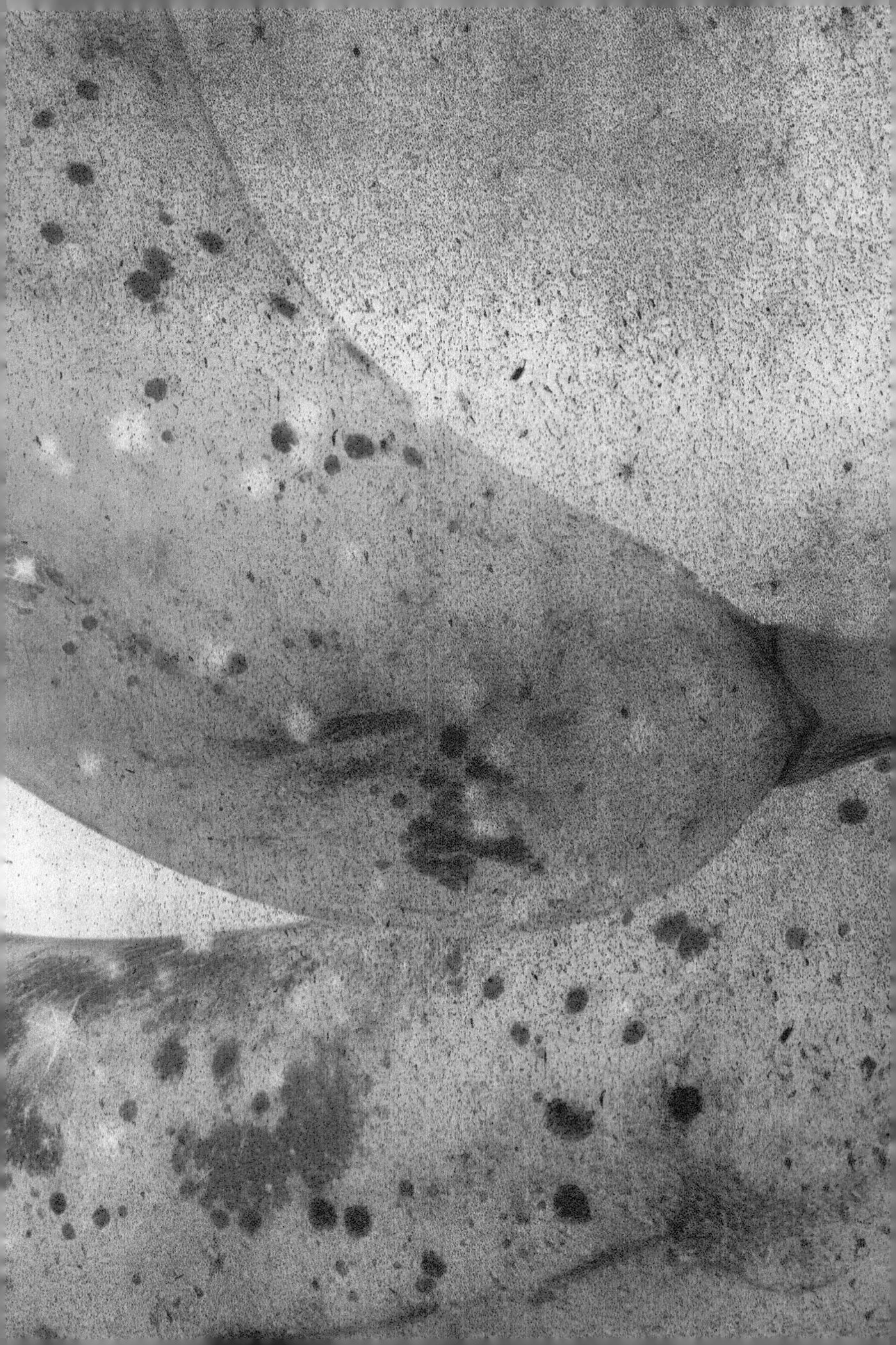

"Let the wolves howl"

Coldplay

Chapter 46

Chapter 47

Adam ran. Harder than his lungs wanted, harder than his legs could carry him.

The revolver was tight in his hand, fear pressing against his ribs like a second heartbeat.

Somewhere in the distance, Emma's voice echoed through the megaphone like a biblical calling.

"Dilly, if you can hear this, your Uber is here." The absurdity landed like a lifeline. She kept going, her voice bouncing off cages and brick and bone.

"To the tiger roaming free, you are majestic, but please don't eat us."

"Hey animals, guess what? Fucking Adam Holcomb thought he should kiss me tonight. What a loser!"

"Animals of the Prescott Zoo, tonight the humans are locked in with you."

"Yo bitches, I am the ghost of Steve Irwin, and I command you animals to be chill."

It was ridiculous. It was perfect. It made all of it feel barely manageable. Like maybe this wasn't a suicide mission after all.

Adam saw the facility ahead. One light on inside, glowing like a beacon in the dark. A lighthouse at the edge of a nightmare. He reached the door, breath ragged, and yanked the zoo keys from his pocket. They clanged together, loud in the awful stillness, every wrong key, a prayer slipping through shaking fingers. Just as he found the right one . . . he felt it.

Something large had approached his shadow from behind. The bear? A tiger? Dilly? Then came the voice.

"Drop the gun, fuckhead."

Adam froze.

The revolver fell from his hand and hit the ground with a soft clunk.

He turned slowly, hands rising, confusion tightening in his chest.

Detective Stover stepped into view, pistol raised, eyes locked on Adam like a hunter finally cornering his kill. The keys still hung from the lock. One twist away.

"Sir, I'm not going to hurt you," Adam said, moving away slowly. "I'm just looking for a chimpanzee." In the distance, Adam could still hear Emma shouting. But her calls changed from deranged animal calls to, "Adam, where are you?!"

Stover's head tilted, hearing the name over the megaphone. "You Adam?" he said, knowing he found his target now.

"Yes, sir."

"Nephew to Jeff Harrison? Brother to Ruby Holcomb?"

Adam blinked, caught off guard. "Yes. How do you—"

"Don't move," Stover said, stepping closer. "You're under arrest for the murder of Lena Wiles."

"What? Lena? What the hell are you talking about?" Adam shouted, his voice rising, his body turning just enough to plead his case. It all happened too fast for Adam to call out. He didn't see the wolf until it was already on him. Instinct screamed: *Don't move. Don't let it know you're here.* Gus, the zoo's alpha male launched from the darkness and grabbed the detective by his shoulder, dragging him to the ground. Stover barely made a sound before the wind was knocked out of him on his way down with a thud.

Small moans and grunts could be heard beneath the snarls. Then came the first rip. The wolf's jaws clamped on his cheek with a sound like wet slop. Stover's scream followed—high, human, and short-lived. The wolf didn't stop. It went lower, tearing into his thigh. Muscle peeled from bone like meat off a stick. Stover spasmed. Sobs cut through the night.

"Help me!" he cried.

There was a moment when he locked eyes with Adam.

Adam could have shot the pistol into the air, kicked the wolf, or drawn attention. He didn't.

Silent gray shapes emerged from the dark like smoke with teeth. No barking, just instinct and intent. Emma's megaphone meant nothing now. The scent of blood cried louder. Adam backed toward the door, slipped the key into place, and snuck into the medical facility.

He left Stover to die.

A feeling he hated more than himself.

But he let the sacrifice to unfold. A grim trade for a story he had to finish. Whatever was necessary for Ruby.

Whatever necessary.

But I miss you
But there's no comin' home
There's no comin' home
With a name like mine
I still think of you
But everyone knows
Yeah everyone knows
If you care then let it go

Coldplay

Adam stepped into the room and immediately felt the temperature drop.

Not cold, just old. Familiar.

The light above him in the facility flickered once, then stilled, as if the world he was a part of went to sleep and another awoke. Even the clock on the wall seemed to give up, its red second hand paused mid-tick, unsure whether the time was still worth keeping here.

Then the humming started. Like the way the ground shakes before it opens itself and swallows what walks upon it.

Only, this hum didn't come from the ground, the walls, or the vents. It vibrated somewhere behind his ears, inside his own skull, like his brain was tuning to a different frequency.

The room shimmered, the way air does above a flame. The way logic bends in a dream.

Adam watched how the white sterile walls began to peel like yellow fruit. The room wasn't collapsing. It was ripening. The sterile floor melted into damp grass. The walls stretched and groaned like a giant waking from hibernation.

Then, everything collapsed inward, and open sky took its place. Where the gurneys and cabinets had stood, there were now rows of folding chairs perfectly aligned.

At the front: two caskets Identical. Polished.

Adam knew this place. He'd been here before.

Not a premonition. A ghost.

The wind smelled like lilac and loss.

His parents' funeral.

Pastor Abraham stood before the crowd, skin dark and freckled, white beard hairs jutting like bent staples. His lips moved, but the words were muffled, gurgled, as if he spoke through a mouthful of slop.

Adam walked the aisle. He'd done this before. A hundred times in his head. A thousand in his dreams. This time, the banana boy pushed through. He reached for the pastor, and his hands passed right through him like smoke.

He braced himself at the caskets.

It wasn't them.

It was him. And Ruby in the other.

Adam staggered back and screamed. Not in fear, but understanding.

He wasn't mourning his parents anymore. He was mourning the boy who had promise. The one alcohol and guilt had buried alive. The grief of realizing his bullshit had been killing Ruby. He was at their own funeral, and no one came, except one. A chimpanzee in the back row. Adam's gaze rose to it.

The grass beneath his feet turned to blackened banana peels, soft and slick. He tried to speak, to pull himself out, but the sky cracked. The caskets shook, as if something was trying to crawl out. The dream shredded.

Hell and zoo collided.

He was back.

His phone buzzed in his hand.

Three missed calls from Emma.

One text:

> WHERE ARE YOU??? Fifteen minutes is up, I'm calling the cops

Adam stared at the screen; its glow was less a warning and now more a eulogy. Something vital inside him sagged as his plans dissolved. Another attempt at heroism, evaporated like vapor.

Adam's fingers blurred at the edges, soft, damp, browning like overripe fruit. They were sinking into the phone screen. His touch was no longer human, with bone and blood. It was spongy. The sweet and sour rot was everywhere, or maybe just in his mind.

Victory was gone.

The supernatural had already peeled him down to the banana bone.

Jeff sat alone in the back of the cruiser, abandoned in the darkness. Stover had bolted toward the zoo gates pistol ready, swallowed by the night. Rage and fear jostled inside Jeff's chest. The steel cuffs chewed into his soft wrists. Bone felt like putty, or maybe like it was already rotting. A distant scream scraped the night, brittle and feminine, distorted by the hot wind. Jeff pressed his ear against the scorching glass to catch words, but only a ragged echo reached him. He didn't give a shit anymore if the zoo burned to ash. Or if Arizona opened its mouth and swallowed it whole.

Then it began.

A tightening in his spine.

A hot pressure behind the eyes.

The suffocating certainty of being watched.

Not noticing. Not curious. Judging.

Something in the very near distance waited with patience and intent. It was the kind of gaze that didn't come from human eyes. A rotten feeling slid under his skin like sewage, and for the first time, he wondered . . . Is this what they felt?

The girls.

The kids.

His mother.

The ones he watched from behind doors, through glass, in black secrets. This creeping, claustrophobic awareness that something was out there, studying you with no face or no soul. Jeff now knew, it wasn't just that he was being watched. It was that whoever, or whatever, was watching him had known what he'd done. Was it Detective Stover? Was it Ruby?

A shape emerged under the zoo's buzzing marquee. First, yellow eyes. Then, a staunch silhouette standing upright.

Daffodil.

The chimp's grin gleamed, teeth catching the neon, and bile surged in Jeff's throat.

"The fuck," he whispered to no one.

Daffodil marched toward the cruiser, arms swinging. Something dangled from his fists. Twisting, writhing lengths . . . ropes? Vines? Snakes. Scales glinted under the parking-lot lights.

Jeff recoiled, cuffs carving fresh grooves.

Daffodil pressed his snout against the glass, breath fogging a circle between them, eyes gloating.

Jeff kicked at the partition, shrieking, but the steel cage did not budge. The chimp knew it wouldn't.

Tap. Tap. Tap.

Dilly's face pressed harder. Glass cracked under the pressure. Jeff's heartbeat drummed.

A latch clicked.

"No, no, no, he begged."

A devil-to-devil prayer for mercy.

Daffodil hurled three coiled rattlesnakes onto Jeff's lap and slammed the door shut. Scales rasped against vinyl; tails rattled like broken buzzers. Fangs punched his flesh. Venom burned a path through his muscle, fire one moment, ice the next. Jeff's scream curdled into wet gurgles as every heartbeat pumped poison deeper. Outside, the chimp watched, fogging the glass with each satisfied exhale.

Jeff's vision tunneled.

He tried to scream one last time, but the snakes had claimed his final breath.

Judgment had come.

"A warning sign
You came back to haunt me"

Coldplay

Chapter 48

Chapter 49

Emma kept screaming into the megaphone, her voice cracking in the humid chokehold of the reptile house. The air was thick and reptilian, baked hot by the red heat lamps overhead. Everything smelled like soil and sweat. Around her, the glass in the terrariums was fractured or shattered. Frogs, gone. Turtles, vanished. Snakes, missing. She didn't care where they went. Not tonight. Except for one thing . . . the rattlesnakes. The thought brushed the back of her mind like a whisper she didn't want to hear.

Three minutes passed.

She stared at her phone, tracking time like it was a lifeline.

Then she shouted again, louder this time, into the red glow and darkness.

Anything that came to mind. Childhood jokes. Stupid threats. Even the voice of Steve Irwin, half-hearted and tired. She screamed things that might make her smile in any other moment, trying to fool herself into thinking she wasn't standing in a room filled with loose predators and broken glass.

Seven minutes.

No message.

No ping.

Adam should've texted by now.

Keep screaming. Stick with the plan. You're safe in here, she lied to herself.

Nine minutes.

She tried calling.

No answer.

Something shuffled behind her.

A scrape.

A soft crunch.

She spun, body stiff with adrenaline, breath shallow. The shadows stretched deep beneath the red lamps and nothing looked real anymore.

Ten minutes.

Another call.

No answer.

"Fuck!"

Her voice broke as she shouted into the mega-phone. "Adam, where are you!"

Her echo bounced off the walls and died near the snake enclosure. Leaves rustled again. The hellish red light left everything half-seen, half-nightmare.

Emma slid along the time, back to the wall, loading the tranquilizer rifle with shaking hands.

Her skin stuck to the metal stock.

Her voice was nearly gone.

Her mind began to wander to escape the fear: she wished she'd kissed Adam. She wished she'd never taken this job. And wished she'd never met the banana boy.

Twelve minutes.

Her throat burned.

Her courage drained.

Then came the knock.

One tap. Then another. Then another.

Knock. Knock. Knock.

Someone knew she was in there.

Bears didn't knock.

Cops hadn't been called.

Adam would have burst through the door, not knocked.

Fourteen minutes.

"Fuck this," she muttered, dropping the megaphone, grabbing her phone. She called 911 with trembling hands. Her voice was raw, barely human, but she prayed the operator understood enough to take her seriously. Knock. Knock. Knock. Knock. Knock.

Five times now. Firm. Unchanging. Emma called Adam again.

Nothing.

She texted him. *Time is up.*

Hell is here.

Then the banging began.

Nonstop.

Glass rattled, reptiles scattered.

The door swung open, hinge moaning.

And there he was.

Mark.

Her ex-husband.

The man who left her for making a life-altering decision without him. The man who said, "I'll never forgive you."

The man who cried harder than any man should, squeezing her in grief.

"Mark?" she whispered, lowering the dart gun as her face leaked.

Then he began to peel.

Hands tore into his own face like wrapping paper. Skin stretched and tore, falling in long red strips.

Muscle unraveled like wet cloth.

Veins popped like cords. Hair, sharp and coarse, bristled from the inside.

Eyes rolled back, then forward again, glazed yellow like wax fruit.

Blood dripped from his chin in long ropes.

Meat flapped off his chest and hit the tile like a butcher's slurry. And there stood Dilly, breathing deep.

Emma raised the rifle, shooting one dart in the chest. Her second shot went wide. Dilly walked in slowly on two legs, shutting the door behind him. Emma screamed, not a name or a word, just a purely animalistic howl. She fired the last dart into his thigh. No reaction.

The chimpanzee came closer. They were alone now. One screaming. One listening. The screaming stopped first.

Fifteen minutes had passed.

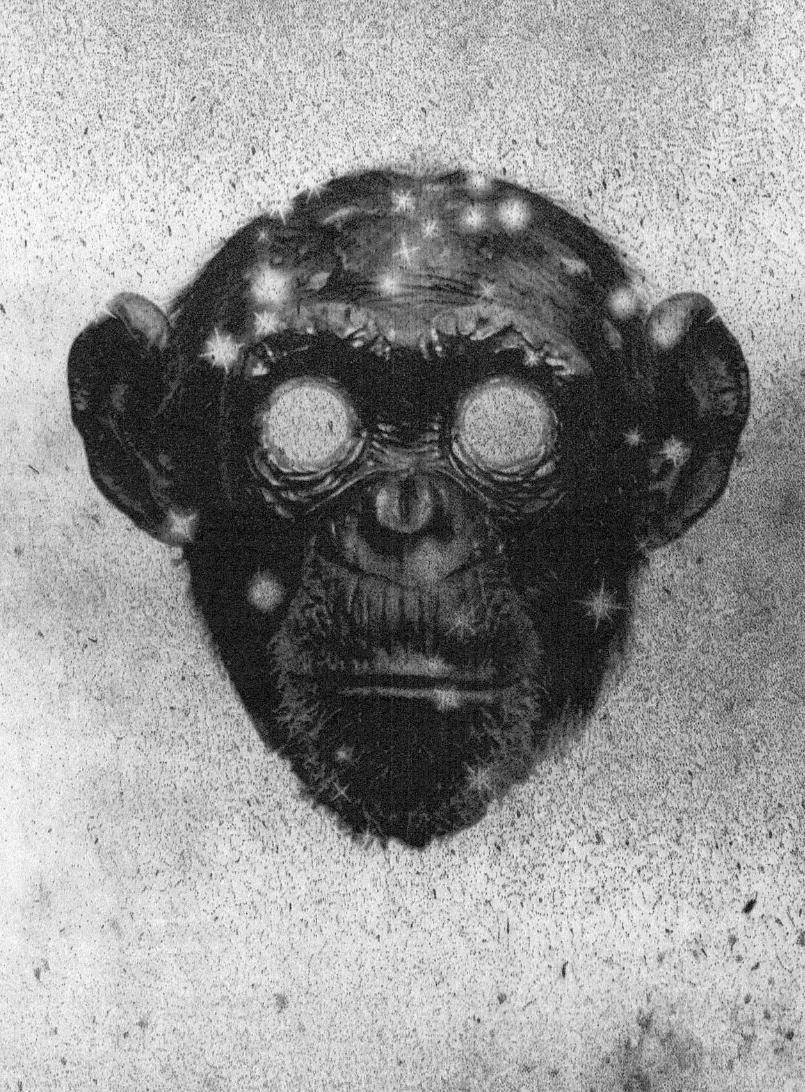

"Oh brother I can't I can't get through
I've been trying hard to reach you
'cause i don't know what to do
Oh brother I can't believe it's true
I'm so scared about the future and I wanna talk to you
Oh I wanna talk to you"

Coldplay

Chapter 49

Chapter 50

The medical facility was empty.

No Dilly. No sign of where he went.

Adam knew what that meant.

He had to go back out there.

But now the cops were there to shut him down.

And somehow, in some lunacy, he was the prime suspect in Lena's murder. He didn't even know Lena was dead. The name slammed around his skull, igniting a fire behind his eyes. The ricocheting bullet of hopelessness bounced inside him.

He wanted to walk back to Emma.

He wanted to run toward Ruby.

He wanted to put a gun to his temple.

He couldn't think straight. His brain blistered, trying to hold too much.

Then he heard it.

"Adam!"

He turned toward the door.

"Adam!"

It came again. Desperate. Raw. Not an echo, a scream that cracked something in him open. He could feel the ricocheting bullet fly through the cracks.

"Adam, help me!"

Ruby!

Somehow, she was here, in the zoo, in the middle of all this chaos.

Adam bolted to the door and peeked through the cracked frame.,

The wolves were gone.

Only a shredded human mass of pulp and fabric remained. His stomach lurched as he tried to make out what was face and what was innards. Even now, a couple of months later, blood still triggered the same sickness that had first rooted itself after the accident.

"Adam!" Ruby's voice again, panic sharpening her voice.

Adam tracked the sound west, toward the chimpanzee enclosure that sat at the top of the ravine.

He tried calling Emma.

No answer.

He texted:

> Heading toward the chimp enclosure. I hear Ruby! I still have time! Meet me there?!!?

No ellipsis.

No response.

The voice in his head told him Ruby's voice wasn't just fear.

It was terror.

He scanned the outside grounds for the fallen pistol. Gone, kicked away, or swallowed by the dark.

It didn't matter.

He had no more time.

Adam launched forward, sprinting.

He ran like something was hunting him.

He ran like freedom waited ahead, even though he knew the devil waited patiently with chains. The zoo blurred around him. Broken fences, overturned trash cans, shadows moving where they shouldn't.

The chimp enclosure loomed ahead, front gate wide open like a mouth.

No lock. No hindrance. Just welcome.

"Ruby?!" he shouted, chest heaving.

"Adam?"

Her voice, high and distant from the upper ridge of the habitat.

He looked up.

A pale, flickering, blue glow pulsed in the dark like the cold eye of some alien cyclops. An iPhone screen, blinking through the silhouettes of the night.

It watched him.

It beckoned the banana boy to his climax.

Everything inside Adam unraveled.

A reckoning climax rose, a scream caught in the throat of the night. A fire ignited in him, the will to fight, to confront a fury he didn't know he carried.

He bolted uphill toward Ruby's cries, his lungs burning, feet pounding the fake jungle dirt.

Dead chimpanzees littered the ground like forgotten puppets—some missing jaws, others hands—every one twisted into shapes no body should ever take.

His gut clawed at him, *Run. Be the coward you've always been.*

The farther he climbed, the more ruin he saw.

Flashes of the accident bolted through his heart and mind.

This wasn't a cage anymore . . . It was a graveyard.

A desecrated temple of meat and madness.

And still, he ran.

At the summit, Dilly stood like a statue against the rising moon in the distance. In his grip, Ruby.

Her body dangled, limp, but alive.

Her skin swollen and purple, breath shallow, one eye swollen shut, the other just barely open.

She was conscious.

She smiled, or maybe it was a reflex.

"Dilly," Adam said, voice low and cracking. "I know you understand me. I know you're not just an animal. But please stop."

Dilly didn't answer.

He didn't need to.

He simply extended his arm farther, lowering Ruby over the edge.

Her scream sliced the air like a knife.

"Stop!" Adam cried, stepping back with his hands up.

"Okay. Fine. What do you want from me?"

The arm holding the phone didn't waver.

Hands slick with apple-red blood. The contrast between the blood and the screen was electric. The phone glowed in the dark, lighting the red dust coating Adam's sweat-soaked skin.

Then Dilly shifted, turning the phone toward Ruby. She groaned as she shifted in the animal's grip, her eyes fluttering. He jolted her, a quick shake, and she blinked herself back into awareness.

She saw it too.

The photo.

Adam didn't need to look.

He saw it in her face.

He knew exactly what Dilly was showing her.

Something caved in Adam's chest.

Maybe the death of a human heart.

Guilt exhaled.

"Adam," Ruby whispered, her voice breaking. "What am I looking at?"

Adam's hands lifted slowly, open and bare. Surrender poured from his posture. "I'm sorry," he said.

The words broke apart in his mouth.

"Ruby, I'm so sorry."

Hot wind picked up again.

The phone screen burned between them like a sacred flame.

"When the tears come streaming down your face
Cause you lose something you can't replace
When you love someone, but it goes to waste"

Coldplay

Chapter 50

Chapter 51

The Diamondbacks were playing the Dodgers.

A game Adam and Ruby's parents had circled on their calendar for months. Not because they were die-hard fans. Sports were just the background music to the real event: cocktails, catered snacks, and a skybox view that their marketing agency connections paid for.

Adam was home from CalArts for the summer, and his parents wanted to celebrate their boy chasing his dreams in animation and design in the Golden State. They were proud. Genuinely proud. But California hadn't been kind to their son. Adam wasn't thriving . . . he was drowning.

He was failing all his classes and not doing well on his own in the large city. He'd started running with the wrong crowd of people who stemmed from wealthy families and lived with what seemed like immortality. Nothing could touch them.

Adam could not keep up. Getting into this school, in this state, at this time, meant his parents working overtime. Sacrificing vacations and weekends to help pay tuition. But the loneliness of California and the failure to launch meant Adam eventually turned to self-medicating to sustain himself. That medication was alcohol. Dr. Jim Beam was his physician.

By the spring semester of his freshman year, Adam had started drinking more than a liter a day, just to fall asleep. His grades dropped to failing, and his absences stacked up.

By the time summer came, he was already unraveling. That morning, Ruby had been dropped off at a sleepover. Adam had passed out sometime after sunrise, face-down in his sheets, the last drops of bourbon still clinging to his teeth. At noon, his parents woke him gently, thinking he was just a tired college kid. He wiped his face with cold water and blasted some mouthwash. Mask back on. This would be the worst day of Adam's life.

"Here," his dad said, tossing him a Diamondbacks cap.

"Dude, I really don't want to wear this," Adam replied, half-laughing.

"Come on, just for today. Pretend you still miss Arizona," his dad said. "For me and your mom."

Adam bent the bill and put it on, nodding. He could pretend. For them, he could pretend.

Then came the keys.

"You're driving," his dad said.

"Dad, I'm tired. I'd rather not."

"Oh, come on, it's not that far."

"I'm wiped," Adam said again, eyes hollow.

His mom stepped in with a grin. "Tell him, Alan."

"Tell me what?" Adam asked.

His father beamed. "It's yours. The 4Runner. We're giving it to you."

Adam blinked.

He washed that car every weekend in high school. Obsessed over its curves like a crush. It had been his chariot. And now it was fully his.

"You're serious?"

"We saved up for a new one. And hey, it's a tax write-off," his dad joked, pulling him into a hug.

The sunlight broke through Adam's haze. Just for a moment.

"I guess you want to drive now," his mom said, climbing into the backseat.

The three of them drove to Chase Field Stadium, Adam reveled in his new gift, bourbon still whispering in his blood. His father put on Coldplay, air-guitaring and singing from his gut. From the backseat, his mother fumbled with her phone for a selfie. But couldn't get the right angle to capture all three of them.

"Here, I'll take it," Adam said, one hand on the wheel.

They smiled. Three faces, bright in the Arizona light.

That was the last smile they would ever share.

The truck came fast.

An eighteen-wheeler cut into their lane like a wall of metal.

Adam twisted the wheel too hard, too fast.

The tires screamed.

The car flipped.

Sky. Earth. Sky. Earth.

Metal folding. Glass breaking into stars.

The SUV spun like a top as if the world forgot up from down.

No screaming.

Just the radio playing.

Coldplay, mocking the wreckage. A happy song covering life in black paint. Adam's skull hit the window hard, cracking the glass.

He watched his mother fly around the vehicle as her seatbelt hung loose from the selfie attempt.

Blood and specs of car glass painted the inside of the vehicle. As quickly as it happened, it stopped.

The SUV was a hundred feet away from the freeway, a smoking casket. Adam moved, unbuckling himself upside down and falling to the ceiling of the car.

"Mom! Dad!"

Smoke.

Silence.

His father groaned, his face purpled and shredded.

His mother didn't move. Her frame collapsed like crumpled tin foil.

"Adam," his father rasped.

"Switch."

"What?" Adam whispered, blood coming from his lips.

"Switch," he repeated, gripping Adam's collar.

With fading strength, he pulled his son across the front seat, dragging himself into the driver's side.

"Dad, no," Adam begged, confusion thick in his throat.

But it was done.

The passenger door opened.

Strangers pulled Adam from the wreckage, limbs flailing like a newborn torn from the womb.

He cried out for his parents. His arms stretched back into the twisted gift that had become a curse. His voice cracked with a grief the heavens wouldn't forgive. Questions that would haunt him like a specter. *Was he still drunk from the night before? Was it all just an accident? Was it the misdirection and distraction?*

The last good and worst thing he ever did with his parents was take that photo. Frozen and smiling.

Unaware.

Knowing everything.

And now it was in the hands of something that wasn't supposed to exist. A chimpanzee with yellow eyes and human habits.

A photo molested by fingers too intelligent.

A photo stared at like scripture.

"You're so far away
Oh, you're so far away"

Coldplay

Chapter 51

Chapter 52

"Do you think when I die, I'll go to heaven?" Ruby asked softly, licking the stringy remnants of greasy Peter Piper Pizza cheese from her bottom lip.

The question didn't match the setting.

It hit sideways, more like something random than serious. Adam didn't look up. His thumbs moved across his phone screen like it was a shield.

"You go to heaven if you believe in Jesus," he muttered, barely registering the words. Distraction felt safer than discussion. It always had.

Ruby set her half-eaten slice down, untouched since her first bite. "Yeah . . . but I don't know if I believe in Jesus." That made him glance up. Not all the way. Just enough to read her face, see how serious this really was. He scanned her like a battlefield medic, trying to guess how deep the wound really went.

"All I remember from Sunday school," he said slowly, "is that it's not about being good or bad. It's about believing in Jesus' goodness, or something like that."

Ruby blinked. "So . . . Hitler could be in heaven?"

Adam rubbed his temple, giving a forced smile. "I don't know. But . . . I heard Jeffrey Dahmer is. That guy got baptized in prison. Repented or whatever. So yeah. If heaven's real, and if Jesus is who He says, I guess you could end up sitting next to him." Ruby's eyes dropped like stones, staring through the table like it was made of glass. Adam felt her pull away, emotionally and spiritually, and he knew he'd just failed as a big brother. Again.

"Why are you asking about this? You're young, you've got a very long time before you die."

She didn't answer right away. When she did, her voice cracked like dry earth. "Do you think Mom or Dad believed in Jesus?" Ruby asked, her words hit Adam like a bat to the skull. All the questioning finally caught up to his distracted brain. Ruby stood from her side of the purple Formica booth.

She didn't look angry, she didn't cry. Just walked around to Adam's side and then folded into him like a child remembering she could still be one. Her face pressed into his chest, hot and silent. Her eyes were red, redder than the Arizona soil. But there were no tears. Just mourning the unknowable pain of what's and why's. Adam felt his insides grow heavy as his sister burned into him. He knew he was the cause of this, wanting to purge himself of guilt.

But he couldn't.

He knew someday he would but today wasn't that day. And if that day ever comes, it would set both him and Ruby free.

Someday.

"For some reason I can't explain
Once you go, there was never, never an honest word
That was when I ruled the world"

Coldplay

Chapter 52

Chapter 53

They could all hear the sirens in the distance.

That was the only sound, until Adam lanced the fear-boil that had been festering like a pus infection since that fateful day.

"Ruby . . . I need to tell you something.

And I need you to hear it, even if you never speak to me again. Even if it breaks everything.

Because I should've told you forever ago, and I didn't.

I was too much of a coward. I didn't want to lose the only person I had left.

He pulled me into the passenger seat.

Dad moved me.

He switched our seats so it would look like he was driving. But, I was the one driving, Ruby. It was me the whole time. Me and my hungover, drunken stupid self.

He knew what it would mean for me if they found out.

How I'd be taken away, how life would just be . . . over."

Adam's words could barely get through the weeping.

"Rubes . . . even as Dad was dying, he tried to protect me. And I let him. I let him take the blame. I let everyone believe the lie. And you want to know the truth? I wanted him to. I wanted my life to be clean, and untouched. Then I watched you cry and ask all the questions . . . and I said nothing. Because I didn't know what to do. Do I let our dad's final act carry on? Or do I . . . undo what—?"

Adam's chest hitched.

I'm not saying this to be forgiven. I'm not even saying it to make things right. I'm saying it because you deserve the truth. I've been fucking lying to you like a coward in every way. I'm so, so sorry, Ruby."

Adam saw Dilly lift its primal snout into the dry, desert air, tasting the confession like ashy flakes from a fire. In that moment, Adam felt the weaver flip the tapestry: the chaos, the meaning, the punishment.

Sirens were closer now.

Radios squawked.

Shouts carried on the wind.

Ruby looked up from the photo, her swollen face softening. Tears rivered over her broken features.

"I found them!" a cop shouted at the bottom of the chimp habitat.

"I would trade everything," Adam sobbed.

"Anything. My fucked up future, my breath, my whole damn life . . . to just go back and undo what I did. But I can't. And I've hated myself for it every day since. And it took this nightmare to finally say it. Our parents are dead because of me."

Ruby opened her mouth to speak.

But before her voice could find shape, Adam turned toward the monster.

"Switch."

That word.

It had stalked Adam through every nightmare since that cursed day, scratching within his skull like a rat.

But now, in the blood-wet silence of this moment, it was the only word that felt hopeful. The animal's head ticked sharply to one side, as if something behind its eyes was rebooting. Calculating the banana boy's request.

"Switch," Adam said again, louder now.

"Let me switch with her. Please!"

Behind him, Ruby started to whimper.

Adam didn't look back.

He didn't have to.

He could feel her breaking.

She opened her mouth, maybe to curse him, maybe to scream, maybe just to breathe.

The words trembled behind her teeth, forged in betrayal, fury, and the raw truth. But they never made it out.

Before her voice could claim the moment . . . Dilly let go.

He didn't shove. He simply opened his fingers, and Ruby slipped from his grip like a drop of blood. Her body twisted in midair, arms flailed for something that wasn't there.

No scream. Just wind and gravity.

Adam's eyes went wide as the horror unfolded in slow motion.

His arm reached out, as if love could break physics. "Ruby!!!"

He barely got the word out before bodies crashed into him from behind.

Police drove him into the dirt, knees and elbows grinding him down.

"Get off me! No! Ruby!" he shouted, thrashing under them, eyes locked on the ledge.

"Ruby!!!"

Dilly stepped back.

The phone fell from his hand.

It clattered against the rocks, glass shattering, image flickering before fading to black. That would be the last time he saw that photo. Then Dilly dropped to all fours.

Spine rippling.

Arms bent.

The mock-human posture melted away, like an actor bowing after the final act. He was an animal again. Or maybe he always had been?

Adam screamed again, voice cracking into sobs, his mouth filled with red dirt, spit, and grief.

"Ruby!"

His body shook hard against the cuffs. "Ruby!!!"

The only answer was the hoot and grunt, from the chimpanzee pretending to be a chimpanzee.

Everything Adam had ever loved was gone.

"And in the end, we lie awake.
And we dream of making our escape"

Coldplay

Chapter 53

Chapter 54

The two detectives entered the room as if they'd just come off a smoke break and couldn't be bothered to pretend this wasn't routine.

One was peeling a banana.

The other was gripping a Styrofoam coffee that steamed against the flickering fluorescent light above.

They didn't rush.

They didn't speak.

They just dropped into their chairs like men who knew the furniture better than their families. The banana peel hit the metal table with a wet slap, folding over itself like something already dead.

Adam stared at it, unmoving.

He was covered in dirt and dried blood, his shirt torn at the collar, wrists cuffed to the table.

His eyes looked hollow, as if the life had been emptied from them, a light that had burned out hours ago.

"You feel like talking truth now?" said the one with the banana, leaning forward, elbows on the table like it was poker night.

Adam didn't respond right away.

He'd already told them everything.

About the supernatural monkey.

The photo.

Emma's apartment.

Ruby.

He knew saying it out loud sounded like a hundred pounds of bat shit—but he was done lying.

"Did you search the ravine?" he asked quietly, voice cracked and low, like it was coming from under a pile of ash.

"Yeah," said the coffee drinker, flipping through a file without looking up. "Our guys are still out there. Nothing yet."

"We went through it. Clean. No signs of a young woman. You sayin' we missed something?"

"I'm telling you the truth," Adam whispered.

He wiped at his face with one cuffed hand, the other dragging behind it like dead weight.

"I'm not making any of this up, Emma can vouch for it all," Adam said with the conviction wobbling between desperation and self-doubt.

"Once this Emma shows up, we'll let you know."

"She was in the reptile house," Adam blurted.

Words tumbled over each other.

"Did you even look? She could be hiding behind the tanks, or at another part of the zoo, or, or—"

The two officers traded a glance, the kind that locked out civilians and buried truth. They already knew what the reptile house had offered up.

"We are collecting evidence from the scene," the senior cop said, voice like gravel. "When she turns up, then she can verify your alibi."

The banana detective leaned back, letting out a long breath.

"Here's what we do have: An overcooked dog in an oven. A missing girl. A murdered woman. Photos of her on your phone. Threatening texts. A house full of shit. Witness statements. Broken zoo security equipment. And now your uncle says it was all you."

"If no Emma, then like I've said a hundred times, ask my uncle, he can vouch for me!" Adam said, readjusting himself as he was trying achieve some control in the chaos.

"Listen," the senior detective said, scratching his sandpaper neck. "We just got final confirmation from our medical examiner. Your uncle has passed."

"What?" Adam asked. He heard the words, but processing failed him.

"Fatal snakebite."

"Snakebite?! How is that possible?"

"We can't disclose much more than that, but we wanted you to know he is gone."

"Where?! How?!" Adam asked as his hands fumbled back to the table. He wanted to argue, to demand details, but no words came. The detectives just sat there, waiting.

"Did you like your uncle?"

"We had our disagreements and differences, but we were family."

"Did you know he filed for guardianship over your sister?"

"No fucking way."

"Way fucking way," the banana cop said, smirking to himself. "The reptiles were removed from their enclosure at the zoo. Their cages broke open. Seems intentional, doesn't it?"

Adam felt the weight of the uncontrollable, the unbelievable stack upon him. Crush him. "You can't be serious?"

"You're in the center of this all, Adam."

Adam shook his head slowly.

Not a denial, just disbelief that any of this was real.

"And then there's Officer Stover," the other detective said.

No edge, just fact.

"One of ours. Dead. This isn't good, Adam."

Adam looked up.

No fight left.

Plastic crinkled.

The cop pulled an iPhone from his jacket pocket, sealed in a cloudy evidence bag. Cracked. Smeared with dried mud. Along one corner, the bite marks were unmistakable, something had tried to eat it.

"We tracked your phone," the officer said, laying it gently on the table.

"It led us straight to this. Right where you were."

Adam didn't flinch. He just nodded, hollow and calm, knowing truth sounded like madness.

Another officer leaned in, voice firmer now. "Are we going to find any more incriminating evidence on this device?"

The phone sat between them like a bomb, ticking with every memory and lie.

Adam stared at it.

That phone had been a weapon, a mirror, a witness. It had seen the truth he could barely stand to carry. His mind raced again. Excuses again. Escape hatches again. But then something gave.

He breathed out, slow and shaking.

Unlocked the iron cage of guilt and shame.

"Yes," he said.

The word landed heavily in the room. But inside him, something released. His shoulders dropped.

The chaos finally quieted. "So now what?" Adam asked, already knowing the answer.

"Now?" The coffee hit the table with a dull thud. "Now you sit. You wait for the arraignment. And unless you give us something real, something we can chase that doesn't sound like a goddamn acid trip, you take the full ride. Your life will be through."

The banana cop leaned forward again, dropping his banana peel on the table in front of them.

His voice dropped low.

"BooBoo the monkey didn't kill anybody. But somebody did. And right now, all signs point to you."

Adam looked past them into the mirror, into his own reflection.

And all he saw staring back was a boy who had lost everything.

The cops stood. Chairs squeaked. Papers rustled. The door closed on Adam's life with a quiet draft. He sat there, shackled under the buzzing fluorescent lights. The banana peel lay limp on the table, discarded and slick. Its curve barely held shape. He stared at it like it might breathe.

Waited.

Watched.

Knowing it could twitch, attack, curl, rise into something it was never supposed to be.

But it didn't.

Not yet.

"Holcomb. Phone call."

"Holcomb!" The officer shouted again, this time with a bang against the bars.

The sound tore Adam from his deep sleep. The voice was sharp and echoing off concrete like a metal pipe dropped in a well. He blinked up from the cot, his chest damp with sweat from another fitful sleep. His cell in the short amount of time he had been there had already been redecorated with illustrations and charcoal renderings of Ruby's face, her smile and the random pencil landscape. It was early and just after shift change, the hour when the prison felt most ghost-like.

He had never received a phone call before . . . not one.

His breath caught in his throat. It had to be his lawyer? Maybe a judge had reviewed something, anything. Or Emma? Maybe she wasn't dead? Maybe she had just vanished and will now reappear? Hell, maybe it was the greatest YouTube prank ever and he was about to get in on the bit? He could feel a rush in his heart and mind. Whoever it was, his prayer was for a new version of grace, a new voice, a new gospel. A resurrection of the life he lost.

He moved fast, sliding into his jumpsuit and jogging down the corridor just outside the cafeteria, toward the yellow wall where the rotary phones sat bolted like fossils. The guard who'd called his name was already there, waiting. He nodded at Adam and placed the receiver gently on the cradle, like he was afraid of it. Adam slowed, catching his breath. "Who is it?" he asked the guard, trying to keep his voice steady. The guard glanced at the phone, then at Adam.

"Said her name's Ruby."

Adam froze.

Time slowed to a drip.

His lungs forgot how to pull in air, as the whole world narrowed to that one impossible word . . . Ruby.

He hadn't heard her name spoken in weeks. Not since the trial began. Not since the paperwork labeled her as deceased or stood in front of men with badges who muttered words like unrecovered remains.

Hope.

It hit him like fire in his veins.

He grabbed the receiver with shaking hands, pressing it to his ear. "Ruby?" he gasped. "Ruby?!"

But the voice that met him wasn't hers.

It wasn't even human.

There was no greeting. Just static, rolling in waves, like the ocean trapped in a distant conch.

Then breathing.

A breathing that came from deep in the chest.

Adam's eyes darted to the guard, but the man had already stepped back, arms folded, watching from a distance as if he'd handed Adam a loaded weapon.

Adam turned his body away from the bars. He spoke again, lower this time. "Who is this?"

The breathing continued.

A slow exhale.

A sharp inhale.

Then something else slithered through the static, a wet whisper inside the wires, a voice he knew but feared to name.

And then it spoke, splitting the silence like a tomb cracking open: "It is finished."

Adam's throat clenched.

The line clicked once.

Then went dead.

Subject: Request for Chimpanzee Following Incident at Prescott Zoo

Hey Bill,

I hope this message finds you well, and you and Lucy are happy and healthy. As you know, I've been placed with P.A.Z for a stint, in light of the recent tragedy that occurred on their grounds.

As you may have heard, they suffered a catastrophic incident last week involving multiple animal enclosures, resulting in several fatalities and significant structural damage. The emotional and operational toll has been overwhelming, and their team is doing everything they can to stabilize both staff and surviving animals. Among those most affected was a male chimpanzee (Daffodil), age unknown, who was housed in the impacted sector. He is the last living primate on location. While he is physically unharmed, his psychological state is deteriorating rapidly due to the trauma and what seems to be an ongoing instability in our facility. In full transparency, after all my years in animal care, this must be the most odd creature I've encountered. During overnight surveillance, Daffodil doesn't move for hours, just stands facing the corner, completely still. Not sleeping but rather staring at nothing. One staff member said she saw him blink in rhythm with the ticking of the security light. With all of that, I'm fearful for his health, Bill.

Given the seriousness of the situation, I'm asking if the Phoenix Zoo would be willing and able to temporarily house this chimpanzee during our recovery period. This place no where close to guaranteeing the environmental safety or staff continuity required for his well-being, and we believe it is in his best interest to be relocated as soon as possible.

We are prepared to handle all transport logistics and provide any documentation or veterinary assessments your team may require. I know this is an unusual and weighty ask, but you owe me one ☺ As well, I trust your leadership and your team's heart for animal welfare.

Please let me know if this is something you'd consider. We're moving quickly to ensure the safety and future of all surviving animals, and I'd be grateful for any assistance Phoenix Zoo can provide during this critical moment.

Golf soon?

Eric Whittaker, Interim Director | Prescott AZ Zoo

www.ingramcontent.com/pod-product-compliance
Lightning Source LLC
Chambersburg PA
CBHW031240310726
48971CB00004B/1098